"Dad, have you and discussed children?"

"We've discussed you kids."

"I mean starting a family of your own."

"I already have a family."

"Esther doesn't."

Tom breathed in a long, cool breath, frowned, then dismissed Ashley's concern. Surely if Esther wanted children of her own, she would have mentioned it by now. The woman hadn't planned to marry at all until he'd come along, let alone have children.

"Dad? Are you still there?"

"Yeah. Listen, the only children Esther and I have discussed are you kids. Don't you think I'd know if she wanted a baby?"

"I don't know. Probably. Sorry for bringing it up."

"All right, I'll be heading over there in a few minutes. Anything I can bring?"

"Just Esther."

"That goes without saying."

"Okay. Love you, Dad. I can't wait until the announcement."

"Me, either."

Tom couldn't shake Ashley's comments as he finished getting ready. He glanced at the baby photographs on his dresser. First Ashley, then Minnie, and finally Chris. For Tom, their childhoods had been filled with the wonder of learning to parent, teaching them the alphabet, that first bike ride without the training wheels. But he had done all of those things alone.

What *if* Esther wanted to have a baby?

TRACEY V. BATEMAN lives in Missouri with her husband and their four children. She sings on her church's worship team and writes full time through the week. Grateful for God's many blessings, she believes she is living proof that "all things are possible to them that believe," and she happily encourages anyone who will listen to dream big and see where God will take them.

To contact Tracey, visit her Web site at:
www.traceybateman.com

Books by Tracey V. Bateman

HEARTSONG PRESENTS
HP424—Darling Cassidy
HP468—Tarah's Lessons
HP524—Laney's Kiss
HP536—Emily's Place
HP555—But for Grace
HP588—Torey's Prayer

Don't miss out on any of our super romances. Write to us at the following address for information on our newest releases and club information.

Heartsong Presents Readers' Service
PO Box 721
Uhrichsville, OH 44683

Or check out our Web site at www.heartsongpresents.com

Timing Is Everything

Tracey V. Bateman

Heartsong Presents

To all my friends and fellow writers from American Christian Romance Writers who are waiting for your "babies" to be born. He truly does make all things beautiful in His time.

Love and gratitude to Chris Lynxwiler and Susan Downs for whirlwind critiques. You two are the BEST!

A note from the Author:
I love to hear from my readers! You may correspond with me by writing:

Tracey V. Bateman
Author Relations
PO Box 719
Uhrichsville, OH 44683

ISBN 1-58660-996-3

TIMING IS EVERYTHING

Our mission is to publish and distribute inspirational products offering exceptional value and biblical encouragement to the masses.

All Scripture quotations are taken from the King James Version of the Bible.

All of the characters and events in this book are fictitious. Any resemblance to actual persons, living or dead, or to actual events is purely coincidental.

PRINTED IN THE U.S.A.

one

The very last thing Esther needed to add to her already frantic schedule was her present conversation with her sister. It wouldn't be so bad if Karen would just say what she meant and then say good-bye so Esther could get back to work. But that wasn't her way—especially when single men were involved.

Resting her forehead against her palm, Esther closed her eyes in a futile attempt to thwart a fast-approaching tension headache. How could she wrap up this call before Karen roped her into another disastrous blind date?

"You've got to meet this guy, Esther. He just started working at the office, and he's so sweet."

Where was that aspirin she'd picked up yesterday? Esther pulled out her top drawer and rummaged around for the plastic bottle while Karen continued to tout the angelic attributes of the latest Mr. Right.

"He's not like the other social workers around here. And oh, Esther, you should just see him with the kids that come into the office. It's just so obvious that he's ready to settle down and start a family. I thought of you right away. Honest, he's perfect for you."

They always are. Esther released a heavy sigh into the receiver and glanced at her watch.

One twenty-five.

"I hate to interrupt, but I'm meeting a new client in five minutes, and my desk looks like a tornado hit it. I need to straighten it up before he gets here."

Never one to take the slightest hint, let alone a direct attempt to say good-bye, Karen continued as though Esther hadn't spoken. "A new *male* client, huh? Is he married? What does he look like?"

"Yes. I don't know. And I don't know. My assistant set up the appointment. To tell you the truth, I've never even spoken with the man."

"Well, make sure you smile while he's there. I just this minute got a feeling about this one."

Karen's "feelings" were legendary—and usually wrong. "You always have a 'feeling about this one.' Besides, what happened to the kid-loving social worker of two minutes ago?"

"Consider him a backup plan in case the new client doesn't work out. Let's talk about your hair. Is it brushed? You'd hate to meet your future husband with messy hair."

Esther patted her hair, which she had painstakingly twisted into a French curl at six-thirty that morning. With a quick glance at the clock, she felt her stomach tense with a desperate need to make a good impression on her new client, male or otherwise.

She debated whether to simply hang up on her only sister and best friend or whether she actually had the patience to have this conversation again. As much as she needed to end the call, she couldn't hurt her well-meaning sister's feelings. But perhaps a little hard-hitting reminder—again—wouldn't hurt. "Listen, Karen, when are you going to get it through your head that I am *not*, I repeat, *not* interested in getting married? *Ever*. Period. I enjoy being alone in my comfy sweatpants and Disney World T-shirt."

"I know, I know. Your perfect date is the Discovery channel and a huge bowl of Rocky Road ice cream. Spare me your diatribe on the benefits of bachelorettehood and how you're married to your career."

Esther chuckled. "I'm not sure bachelorettehood is even a word. As a matter of fact, I'm almost positive it isn't."

"Sure it is." Karen's voice rang with humor. "In Karen's Collegiate Dictionary, bachelorettehood is defined as the state of being an old maid. And your picture is next to the definition in glaring black and white."

"I prefer being thought of as maturely independent. Or independently mature. Either way, I'm happy as I am. And I wouldn't change it for anything in the world."

"You just think you wouldn't change it."

Esther hated Karen's all-knowing tone—the one that spoke of experience that she, Esther, lacked. And why shouldn't it? Karen had found her own Mr. Right during the hot, humid days of her thirteenth summer. She'd never even glanced at another boy after that.

A twinge of jealousy pinched Esther's heart. What would her life have been like if she had found the man of her dreams early in life and had spent the last twenty-five years married and raising children?

There was no time to ponder the probing and troubling question as Karen's lilting voice bubbled through the receiver. "Believe me, Esther, one look at Prince Charming, and you'll turn into a giggling teenager again."

"I was never a giggling teenager to begin with," Esther said wryly. "You're confusing me with you again. Anyway, dear sister, I have to run. My appointment will be here any sec. See you at Dad's on Sunday."

Esther settled the receiver back into its cradle just as her assistant buzzed her.

"Mr. Pearson is here." Thankfully, the nineteen-year-old used her professional voice.

"Thank you, Missy. Send him in."

Esther scowled at the papers scattered across her desk. She

should never have allowed Karen to get her into the "I'm-happily-married-to-my-job" conversation. How in the world would Mr. Pearson ever trust her to keep tidy books if she couldn't even keep her desk clean?

She had thirty seconds—tops—to create the illusion of order from this chaos. Standing, she reached across her desk. Before she could lift a file, her elbow knocked against the large Styrofoam cup half filled with the cold latte she hadn't had time to finish earlier. A stream made a quick run toward her files and papers.

With a cry, she made a mad dash to save the papers. In her despair, she barely heard the door open.

"Uh, excuse me. I'm Tom. Should I come back later?"

"No." Grabbing at a box of tissues on her desk, she attempted to sop up the mess. "Come on in and have a seat," she said without an upward glance. "I'll be with you in a minute."

"Have an accident?"

A groan escaped her lips as the latte found a target. She snatched up the folder and quickly set it out of harm's way. "No, I did this on purpose," she shot back, then gasped and slapped her hand to her forehead. "Oh, good grief. I'm sorry. I just. . .I'm trying to save my papers."

"I completely understand. Here, let me help." His tanned hand, filled with wadded tissue, moved over her desk, sopping up latte. Esther breathed a sigh of relief while the tissue stopped the river from reaching any more papers before she could get them all off the desk. She set the messy, unkempt pile on a nearby file cabinet and settled back into her chair.

"I can finish," she said and, for the first time, glanced up. She caught her breath. "Oh, wow." The greatest-looking Hollywood actors and magazine models were all plastic surgery jobs gone horribly wrong compared to this guy.

Amazingly brilliant blue eyes stared back at her. Never mind that they looked at her as though she might be just a little more than nuts. He was beautiful. Prince Charming meets Andy Garcia.

"Wow?" Prince Andy repeated.

"Huh? Oh, yeah. Wow, that's a messy pile of tissue. Let me throw those away for you. I have a trash can here at my feet." *Great recovery, Esther!* She smiled.

"Here you go." He plopped a sticky, wet mess of soggy tissues into her hand. "Not the kind of gift I usually give a pretty woman."

Esther felt a giggle coming from deep within and was completely powerless to keep it down where it belonged. She was mortified when the offending sound left her lips. Oh, brother. Karen was right. She was acting like a teenager. Time to get control of herself. Much as she hated to admit it, she was forty years old—too old to go crazy over a guy.

"Thank you for your help." She cleared her throat. "Now that that's all taken care of, let's discuss your account."

❧

Tom blinked in surprise at the new personality emerging before him. This enchanting woman had gone from unsure and even a bit ditzy to completely in control in an instant. This personality was probably better for his business, but the other one had made him smile. She hadn't even noticed in all the fuss that one side of her hair was falling from its twisty-knotted style.

"Mr. Pearson?"

He shot a glance back to her eyes.

Her brow arched.

Tom's face warmed at her obvious bewilderment. He'd been staring at her hair, debating whether or not to reach forward and test the shiny strands. They couldn't possibly be as soft as they looked.

She gave him a "snap-out-of-it" scowl.

"I'm sorry. I just couldn't help noticing that your hair is coming loose."

Her amber eyes widened, and she quickly patted her head. "Oh, brother. What next?"

Tom winced as she yanked the pins from her hair and let the rest of her dark tresses flow freely around her shoulders.

A lump formed in his throat, and he could almost feel the silky smoothness of her waves of hair.

"What's wrong?" she asked.

"Nothing. It's just that I've never seen that color of hair before. It's rare."

She snorted. She actually snorted. And to Tom it was an adorable snort. In fact, he wished she'd do it again.

"It's a special blend. Kind of a mahogany slash burgundy. I love it but not enough to call it 'rare' in my hair dresser's presence, or she'll start charging me more." She smirked, and a dimple flashed at one corner of her mouth.

Tom swallowed hard. "Miss Young—"

"Esther."

"What?"

"Call me Esther. That's my name. Unless you'd rather we stay on formal terms."

"No, no. I'm Tom."

"You mentioned that."

A smile tipped his lips. "Esther. I don't usually do this. But, I'm hosting a picnic at the park for the employees of Pearson Lumber this Saturday."

Esther nodded and glanced down at a document on her desk. "I see the cost. It's no problem. You can afford it."

Again, she glanced up at him and smiled.

Tom's returning smile began as a lurch in his heart and sort of exploded onto his lips. "Actually, I'm not telling you about the picnic to find out if I can afford it."

She raised a silky, delicate brow. "What, then?" A look of understanding moved across her features. "Oh, I get it. I'm a new employee and you're inviting me to join the crew."

"Not exactly."

A beguiling pink flooded her cheeks. "I'm sorry, it just seemed like you were building up to an invitation."

Clearing his throat, Tom fought the urge to chuckle. "I'm not very good at this. I'm asking you to come to the picnic. But not as my accountant. As my date."

Wide amber-colored eyes widened farther and her mouth made an "O." "Well, I don't usually—"

"Don't usually go to picnics? Go on dates? Eat barbeque? Mix business with pleasure?"

"That's the one," she said with a wry grin.

"Then, I suppose you'll have to consider yourself fired."

A gasp escaped her lips.

"Just kidding. How about making an exception in this case?"

Tom wasn't sure if she had been shocked into it or not, but pleasure flooded him when she expelled a pent-up breath and nodded. "All right. But don't scare me like that again."

"You have my word. Write down your address, and I'll pick you up at one on Saturday."

Her look became guarded and a slight frown creased her brow.

"Or you can meet me at the picnic," he offered.

"Yes. I'd prefer that. Thank you."

For the next hour, Tom struggled to focus on business while Esther went over his financial statements, making suggestions and praising his financial savvy. Disappointment clutched at him when she stood.

"I guess that's all, Tom."

Was it his imagination, or did she seem sort of reluctant to end the meeting?

She smiled that glowing smile once more, and suddenly moonlight and matching wedding bands flashed through his mind. He shot to his feet, scared to death at his last thought. Or had it been a premonition? A vision from God? A wish? A dream? A crazy hallucination brought on by lack of lunch today? The possibilities were endless. All he knew for sure was that in ten years, since the death of his wife, he hadn't come close to finding a woman interesting enough for so much as a second date, let alone matrimonial intentions.

This woman had certainly piqued his interest. Now it remained to be seen whether she could hold it. He couldn't help but wonder if God might have a second chance at love for him, after all.

Esther walked him to her office door, gave him a sure-handed shake, and promised to see him Saturday at one.

Tom stepped into the sunlight, slapped his Stetson on his head, and sauntered toward his Ford truck, whistling a happy tune.

two

"No, that won't do. Too dressy," Esther muttered to herself.

She tossed the silky, black dress onto the pile of unacceptable clothing accruing on her bed and delved deeper into her closet. There had to be *something* suitable to wear to the picnic. Something that said, "Hey, I might be forty and unmarried, and so far I've liked it that way—but that doesn't mean I couldn't be persuaded to change my mind."

She groaned and sat back on her heels. Time was ticking away. She glanced at her watch to confirm that fact. Only an hour left before she was supposed to meet Tom at the park. How was she supposed to find the all-encompassing outfit, shower, cover her wrinkles, and appear as though she didn't have to work at it in only an hour?

The phone chirped—a welcome diversion. Instinctively, she knew Karen's radar was in full swing. For the past three days, she'd purposely left her beloved sis in the dark about this so-called date because she didn't want to hear the I-told-you-so monologue.

But desperation called for a little humility—the price of Karen's expert clothes advice.

She checked caller ID to confirm her suspicion, then yanked up the phone. "Kare? I need help."

"What's wrong?" Karen's worried voice shot back through the line.

"I have a date in fifty-five minutes and I can't find anything to wear. Don't ask questions; I'll fill you in later. Just tell me what to wear to a picnic!"

"Definitely Levis, your light blue summer sweater, and a pair of slip-ons."

"Hair?"

"Loose. Your hair always flows just the right way. If I didn't love you so much, I'd be insanely jealous."

"Okay. I have to go. I haven't showered yet."

"Wait!"

"What?"

"Don't you want to know why I called in the first place?"

"Sorry. Is everything okay at home? The kids? Brian?"

"Oh, they're fine. I wanted to remind you about your class on Monday."

"Like I could forget my last class." She grinned. After Monday she'd be licensed to become a foster parent. Hopefully, taking care of other people's children would somehow fill the void left by her own childless state.

"All right, one more thing," Karen said. "What was the new client like?"

Esther smirked and rolled her eyes, knowing full well her sister had called with that purpose in mind. The class reminder was only a convenient excuse. "He was passable."

"Passable?" Karen said slowly, as though trying to wrap her mind around what 'passable' could possibly mean. She gasped. "I was *right*. He's your date today, isn't he? I told you I had a feeling about this one."

"Yeah, you're a regular prophetess. I have to get ready."

"All right. Call me when you get home. I want details."

෨

Esther's stomach flip-flopped as she pulled into the car-lined, gravel parking lot. She scanned the humongous park. Four baseball diamonds held little league games in full swing. Six concrete slabs under green aluminum canopies hosted groups of barbequers.

Esther frowned, wondering how she'd ever find the right group. *I should have brought a sign to hold up. Rescue me, Prince Tom. I don't know where I'm going.*

She was about to put the car in reverse and gun it back home, when a knock on her window startled her. She jerked her head around and relief flooded her. Her tall, tanned cowboy stood next to the car, waving. She rolled down the window.

"Hi."

"You made it!" Tom's delighted smile lifted her spirits, effectively erasing the angst of two and a half minutes ago. "I was afraid you might not know which picnic spot to go to. Have you been sitting here long?"

Cute, thoughtful, and unmarried? No one was that perfect. He must live with his mother, own fourteen cats, pick his teeth with his fork. . .something less than desirable. She wasn't lucky enough to hit the jackpot. "I just got here, as a matter of fact."

He offered her his hand like a knight helping a lady from her steed. Sudden warmth wrapped around her as she stood. Inches from his face, she could barely breathe. This combustible chemistry had eluded her in the past.

Was it just imagination fueled by her ticking clock, or could it possibly be that fortune had, at last, smiled upon her? Maybe Cinderella had finally found her prince.

❧

Tom felt like a teenager as Esther slipped her hand into his. He hoped his palms weren't sweaty. How could a woman reaching middle age be as beautiful as any twenty-year-old model—even more beautiful? This woman made every nerve in his body buzz to life.

He kept hold of her hand as they walked toward the picnic spot. It seemed like the natural thing to do, and she didn't protest. He didn't press his luck by lacing their fingers. But the feel of her hand in his felt alarmingly right.

"Thank you for inviting me. I haven't been to a picnic in ages."

Her soft, low-toned voice sent a shiver through him. "My pleasure," he managed around a boulder-sized lump in his throat.

"Where you going, Dad?"

Sixteen-year-old Chris's voice snapped him back to reality. Heat flamed his cheeks as he realized he'd walked a good twenty feet past his group under the canopy.

"Oops," he said, tossing Esther a sheepish grin. "Sorry. This is us."

"It's all right. I'm a little disoriented, too." Her cheeks flooded with pink as if she realized, too late, her admission. He squeezed her hand and turned her loose.

No sense having to explain to the kids why he was holding hands with a woman he'd just met. They were giving him enough of a hard time over this date as it was. And he was the one always telling them to take things slow. How important it was not to skip steps in dating relationships. Now, he wondered how many of those steps he'd skipped by holding hands and thinking long term on the first date.

"Everyone, meet Esther Young, the new accountant."

Chris grinned and stepped forward. "Hi, I'm Tom's son. Are you going to be my new mommy?"

Esther gasped as everyone in earshot chortled.

"Chris, go stuff something in your mouth," Tom commanded. He'd have a talk with the ornery kid later. For now he had to do damage control. His gaze sought his oldest daughter, who sat backward on a picnic table bench. He silently pleaded with her to smooth over Chris's attempt to be funny. Taking the hint, she stood and smiled.

"Hi, Esther. I'm Ashley. Dad's old married daughter. I work in the office as his secretary, so we'll probably be working together some."

Rather than relaxing under Ashley's friendly demeanor, Esther seemed to tense even more. "Nice to meet you," she said tightly.

Tom noticed her gaze shift to Ashley's slightly rounded belly. Was her tension from the realization that he had children or because they were grown? He leaned in close. "Ashley's twenty-two and married to my best contractor, Trevor. They're about to make me a grandpa in a few months."

Esther blanched, her eyes growing wide. "You don't look old enough to be a grandfather."

Or maybe she'd thought him to be younger than he was. Oh, well, no sense putting the truth off. He wasn't ashamed of his age or his status as a soon-to-be grandfather. "I'm forty-five. Ashley was born when I was twenty-three, a year after I married her mom."

"I just turned forty," she murmured. "I suppose, technically, I'm old enough to be a grandparent, too."

As though the revelation was too much for her, she pressed her slender fingers to her collar.

Sensing her desperate desire to bolt from the picnic and most likely from his presence, he used a diversionary tactic. "Can I get you something to drink?"

She darted her gaze to him and wet her lips nervously. "Yes, thank you."

He escorted her to an empty spot at the closest table. "Tea or soda?"

Still looking a little shell-shocked, she stared at him. "Huh?"

"To drink? Tea or soda?"

"Oh, sorry. Anything diet if you have it. If not, unsweetened tea."

A woman who watched her figure. He liked that.

At the drink table, he took a plastic cup of ice. "Hi, Dad. Is that the dish you've been mooning over for the last three days?"

"I haven't been mooning." Tom turned to his middle child, Minnie. The soon-to-be twenty-one year old had that all-wise, all-knowing smirk that usually spelled trouble. Defenses alerted, he gave her a stern look. "Her name is Esther. And you be nice to her."

"I'm always nice." She popped a deviled egg into her mouth and gave him a closed-lip grin, making her pudgy cheeks fill out even more.

"Minnie. . .I mean it. Come and let me introduce you, but don't embarrass the poor lady. Chris already asked her to be his mommy."

Laughter pushed through her lips, and she shook her head, making her blond ponytail wag like a happy dog. "Wish I'd seen that."

Afraid she might try to one-up her younger brother, Tom gave her a stern frown. "I mean it."

She rolled her eyes. "Like I'd embarrass anyone."

Like she wouldn't. Tom grabbed a Diet Coke from one of the ice chests and followed his daughter back to the table. To his relief, Esther and Ashley seemed to be getting along nicely, and Esther seemed to have recovered her poise. He could always count on Ashley to ease any situation. She was like her mother that way.

"Esther, I'd like you to meet my other daughter." He stepped aside and let Minnie move ahead of him. "This is Minnie."

Minnie gave a wry grin and held out her hand. "Yeah, I'm the other one. Chris is the football star; Ashley's the former prom queen and the responsible one. And I'm the fat one. But rather than use that to identify me, we just say 'other.'"

Helpless in the face of Minnie's offended tone, Tom

thought he'd die of embarrassment. Minnie's outburst was worse than Chris's goofing around. But Esther apparently chose to ignore the attitude and took Minnie's hand. Her eyes filled with warmth. "I'm so glad to meet you." She smiled and leaned closer. "Be honest with me. Are there any more of you? Because I have to admit, I didn't know your dad had even one child let alone three."

Apparently still smarting from Tom's lack of a proper introduction, Minnie's eyes narrowed. "Do you have a problem with dating fathers?" The kid was gunning for a fight.

"No," Esther shot back. "If I did, I wouldn't be contemplating asking your dad to see a movie with me after the picnic. Do you have a problem with fathers dating? Yours in particular?"

Silence reigned over the table while everyone waited to see if Minnie would continue to challenge someone who could obviously hold her own in a verbal sparring match. Minnie scrutinized the woman for a second—then gave a tight-lipped smile. "It's not really my decision. He's a grown man. Excuse me. Mitch is waving at me down by the volleyball net." She shot Tom a grin and gave him a thumbs-up.

Esther cleared her throat, obviously as bewildered by Minnie's sudden change in attitude as everyone else around the table. "If Minnie likes you, that settles it," Chris said. "Now you have to be our new mommy. Minnie doesn't like anyone but Ben and Jerry. You know—the ice cream?"

"Yes, I'm aware of them—especially the Rocky Road." She gave a rueful smile.

"Believe me," the boy returned, giving her a glance-over, "you don't know them as well as she does."

"That's enough, Chris." His son constantly berated his sister about her weight. And truth be told, Tom wished she'd take a lesson from Ashley and try to lose a few pounds, but he was smart enough to know that no amount of pushing would do it. She'd lose the weight when she was ready. In the meantime, they had to be sensitive.

Fun and laughter filled the table as the picnickers ate hotdogs and hamburgers and listened to Chris's stories about his recent summer football camp. Esther interjected her own funny stories about her sister and their cheerleading antics. They sat around the table until the sun sank lower in the western sky. Esther's quiet grace and quick humor utterly charmed Tom, and it was obvious she met with hardy approval among his children and employees.

As much fun as the day turned out to be, by the time Ashley declared herself ready to go home and put her feet up, Tom was more than happy to say good-bye and take the opportunity to get Esther alone. "How about a walk around the park?"

"Shouldn't I help clean up?"

"That's the advantage to dating the boss." He grinned. "All you have to do is show up looking gorgeous and let people wait on you."

She still didn't look convinced. Her concern tenderized his heart. "We have these get-togethers four times a year, and we rotate who cleans up. You can get on the list for next time."

She rewarded him with a heart-stopping smile and got up from the picnic bench. "All right. Then I'd love to take a walk."

They set off on a trail cut through a patch of woods at the outskirts of the park. Tom debated whether he could get by with holding her hand but decided against trying. No sense pushing his luck. He'd taken a little advantage of her bad case of nerves earlier. But now there was no good excuse to skip a step.

"I'm sorry I failed to mention the kids when I asked you to come with me today."

In the trooperlike style he was beginning to admire about

this woman, she shrugged. "It was a shock. But there wasn't really time to give each other a rundown of family members. They're great kids." She grinned. "Even Minnie."

He chuckled. "Minnie's a handful. She was only eleven when her mom died. I'm ashamed to say that Ashley has always been a daddy's girl and Minnie was closer to my wife. When Jenn died, Minnie sort of shut down. I didn't know how to deal with her. I'm afraid I still don't."

Esther gave him a sympathetic smile. "She's outspoken but otherwise seems to be a great girl. I bet you're being too hard on yourself." A branch crackled beneath her feet. "Of course I've never been a parent, so I could be wrong."

"Can I ask a personal question?"

She stopped and plucked a handful of Queen Anne's lace from the edge of the trail. "How come a girl like me never got married?"

He chuckled and sidestepped a rut, taking her arm to maneuver her around it. "Something like that."

A breeze blew from the south, lifting her hair up and around her face. She hooked a manicured nail around the invading strands and pushed them away from her face, tucking them behind her ear. Tom was utterly enchanted.

"I guess I just never found the right guy. I had definite goals about my career, and none of the guys I dated really got that about me."

As though unconscious of the effect she had on him, she continued to answer the question while he tried hard to pay attention. But there was this one wisp of hair. . .

Unable to take it anymore, he reached toward her face. She moved back, her eyes wide.

Heat crept to his ear. "Sorry, you have just a strand here." He took it between his thumb and forefinger, marveling at the silky softness.

"Thank you," she whispered, her wide amber-colored gaze captivating him. He rested his palm against her cheek and took a step closer. With a quick intake of breath, she moved back. "I think we may be getting a bit ahead of ourselves."

He nodded and dropped his hand. "You're right. I'm acting like a hormone-ravaged teenager. I hope I'm not offending you."

She sent him an indulgent grin. "It's flattering, actually. But maybe a bit fast. I've been out of commission for a long time."

"Me, too. I'm always telling my kids not to skip steps, and here I am not taking my own advice."

"Well, don't worry," she said wryly. "I'll keep you honest." She cast a glance at her watch, then looked in the direction they'd come from. "I suppose I should get going."

His stomach twisted. He wasn't ready to let her go just yet. "What about that movie?"

"Movie?" She started walking back toward the picnic area. Tom followed.

"You told Minnie you were about to invite me to one."

A low chuckle fell from her lips. "I'm ashamed to admit that I only said that to gain the upper hand."

Disappointment washed over Tom like a cold wave. "I understand. You certainly met your objective. Minnie rarely gets shut down—especially when I've offended her."

"Wait," she said. "I don't absolutely have to go home right now. I'd love to go see a movie with you. But I should warn you, on Saturday nights, I turn into a pumpkin at eleven."

"So early?" Like he should talk. He hadn't stayed up past the ten o'clock news since Chris started kindergarten.

She nodded. "I try to get to bed early on Saturdays so I'm alert for church."

"Where do you attend?"

"Community Bible on Leland Street." She smiled again, her eyes sparkling in the fading light. "It's a huge building. You can't miss it."

Delighted at the welcome coincidence, Tom nodded. "I know. That's where the kids and I attend. Which service do you go to?"

"Eight-thirty. I'm an early bird."

"The kids like to sleep in, so we go to the contemporary service at eleven. It's pretty great."

"I've been meaning to give that service a try. Not because I'm dissatisfied with the more traditional one, but I always listen to contemporary praise-and-worship music at home, and I really enjoy it." She gave a low chuckle. "Besides, I wouldn't mind sleeping in a little."

"You should definitely give it a try. It's more laid back. The kids love it."

She nodded. "I'll do that sometime."

The parking lot loomed ahead of them, and Tom saw that her red mini car and his blue truck were practically the only vehicles left. "So, do you want to ride with me to the movie?"

Her split second of hesitation nearly stopped his heart. Then she smiled, and he was able to breathe again. "I'll meet you over there. That way you won't have to bring me all the way back here afterwards."

"All right." Not that he would have minded the extra time with her.

She turned and unlocked her car door. Tom inhaled her flowery scent, lifted on the wings of another breeze.

"Okay," he choked out as she slid under the wheel. "I'll see you over there."

Climbing into his truck, Tom felt lambasted by the events of the last few days. He'd dated over the years, but his interest in a woman had never lasted any longer than the walk to the door at the end of an evening. Now he felt consumed by a desire to spend more time with Esther.

After ten years alone and raising three children who were pretty much grown, he'd assumed he'd be alone forever once the kids left home. Who would have thought God might have a companion for him to grow old with? A grin tipped his lips. He had the feeling that life was about to get real interesting.

three

Esther stopped at the sanctuary entrance and scanned the seven-hundred-seat room—a futile attempt at finding the proverbial needle in the haystack.

A loud cough over her shoulder caught her attention. She turned and nodded her apology to the tall twenty-something male, who apparently thought he was being discreet in his attempt to inform her that she was holding up traffic.

She moved forward but continued to look for Tom's tall frame and brown hair, peppered with gray flecks. Her heart did a loop-de-loop at the memory of yesterday's date. They'd spent two hours watching a romantic comedy, and she'd been captivated by his genuine laughter during the funny moments. After the movie, they'd gone to a local coffee shop and closed the place down at midnight. So much for turning into a pumpkin at eleven. A smile touched her lips.

"Esther?" a soft voice called from the row of chairs next to Esther. Tom's daughter Ashley moved toward her, looking radiant in a pale green maternity dress. Her dirty-blond hair was cropped short and pushed up in the back. Her eyes, blue like her dad's, sparkled with obvious joy.

"Ashley. Hello." She worked hard not to look past the young woman to see if Tom was anywhere near.

"I've never seen you here before," Ashley said with a lilt in her voice. "Do you want to sit with us?"

Esther nodded, grateful to be out of the aisle. "I usually go to the early service." She slipped into the blue cushioned seat next to Ashley.

"Ahh. That explains it." Her eyes sparked with mischief.

Esther couldn't help but return the grin. "Explains what?"

The girl laughed outright now. "Why Dad went to the early service."

"Are you serious?" Esther joined Ashley's laughter as pleasure sifted through her. This situation was like something out of a movie.

The girl nodded. "If you two are going to be seeing each other, you'd better get your wires straight."

"I suppose you're right." There was no time to continue the conversation as the assistant pastor took the podium and greeted the congregation.

During the high-energy music service followed by a wonderful message, Esther felt her spirit lift to a place she hadn't been in a long time. She couldn't help but wonder if the prospect of new love was renewing her youth.

Ashley gave her a quick hug as they stood. "We'd love for you to join the family for dinner. Dad always makes tons of food on Sundays. Minnie makes dessert and I bring a side dish and vegetable. Today I'm making my famous au gratin potatoes and green beans cooked in sautéed onions and mushrooms."

"Sounds great. You'll have to give me that green bean recipe."

Smiling with more warmth than Esther had ever seen, Ashley nodded. "Come to dinner, and I'll write it out for you."

"Oh, no, I couldn't just drop in on your dad unannounced." The thought horrified her, and even more so because she'd actually taken a split second to consider it.

"Are you kidding? Dad will be thrilled. I haven't seen him really interested in a woman since—well, since my mother, I guess." The girl's tone moved from amused to wistful at the mention of her mother.

Esther touched the young woman's arm as tenderness

surged through her. "I take that as quite a compliment, Ashley. Thank you."

A smile curved Ashley's lips. "It is. My dad's a great man. He did a fantastic job raising us alone. We were always at the top of his list of priorities, which is probably why he never got involved with anyone." Her eyes sparkled. "Until now, that is. I have a good feeling about you."

Esther felt herself coloring. This family certainly didn't hold back. "You should get together with my sister, Karen," she said wryly. "She gets 'feelings,' too."

"I'd love to. We can compare notes." Esther joined the girl's spontaneous and infectious laughter. "Sounds like you and my dad are destined."

"Well, we'll see."

"So how about dinner? I could call Dad if it would make you feel better."

Feeling suddenly stifled, Esther shook her head. "Actually, I have plans today. Some other time, maybe."

Regret slipped over Ashley's face. "Sorry to put you on the spot."

"Oh no. Not at all. I appreciate the invitation, and I look forward to getting to know your dad better." She smiled. "And the rest of you. But I have a standing date on Sundays."

A sudden wariness clouded Ashley's eyes. Her brow arched in question. "A date?"

Esther couldn't hold back a chuckle. "With a very handsome, older gentleman—my dad. And my sister, Karen, and her family."

Ashley's suspicious expression morphed into relief, and she returned Esther's smile. "All right then. May I tell Dad I saw you?"

"Of course. And tell him how polite you were to invite me

to sit with you so I wouldn't feel so awkward." She squeezed Ashley's hand. "I appreciate it."

"It was my pleasure. I hope you'll join the contemporary service again."

"You can count on it."

❧

Later, as she sat in a lounge chair on Karen's deck watching the children splashing about in the spray of the garden hose, Esther closed her eyes and sighed.

"All right now, that's it." Karen's outburst interrupted the tranquility.

Esther squealed as ice chips landed on her bare legs. "Hey!"

"If you don't tell me what's going on in that dreamy-eyed head of yours, I'm going to give the kids permission to hose you!"

"I don't know what you mean," Esther taunted.

"Kids! Aunt Esther's hot! She needs a good cooling off."

"All right!" Ten-year-old Avery turned toward the house.

A sudden spray shot across the deck. Esther sucked in sharply as the cold water made contact with her warm skin. Laughing, she put up her hands in a not-so-successful attempt to ward off the onslaught. "Okay, okay! I give up. Call off your assassins!"

"Okay, kids, I think she's learned her lesson," Karen called to her squealing offspring. "If I need you again, I'll call. Now off with you. Go back to your own games."

"You're a horrible sister," Esther accused with a mock pout, wringing out her once carefully coiffed hair.

Karen tossed her a towel, waggling her eyebrows. "Ve haf vays of making you talk," she said in a poor German accent.

"Oh, please. Okay. I did go to the picnic with Tom yesterday."

"Finally!" Karen plopped into the patio chair next to Esther. "Now, start at the very beginning, and don't leave anything out."

By the time Esther had recounted the picnic, Tom's kids, the hand-holding, the movie, and finally the crossed church services, Karen's eyes gleamed with an excitement that matched the racing of Esther's heart.

"Okay, Esther. So now what?"

"What do you mean?"

"Is he going to call you?"

"I don't know." She wiped away a remaining droplet of water from her tanned leg, trying to appear as though she didn't care one way or another, but her heart didn't want to face the fact that he might not. You just never could tell with men. They all *appeared* to be having a good time. But that didn't necessarily mean anything. But then, he *had* gone to the early service just to be with her. The thought eased some of her angst.

"Well, didn't you discuss if one or the other would call?"

"No."

Giving an exasperated huff, Karen scowled. "He didn't say, 'I'll call ya'?"

A thick cloud of gloom threatened to darken Esther's excitement. Maybe Tom didn't plan to call her, after all. Karen had a point. Wouldn't he have mentioned it if he were going to ask her out again?

"Maybe he saw my desperation and decided the run-don't-walk method of retreat was in order."

"Don't be silly." Karen peered closer and frowned. "How desperate were you?"

Esther tossed the towel at her. "Whose side are you on? You are supposed to reassure me, not add to my fear of rejection."

"Well, you already know that I think you're a real catch. This guy would be nuts not to call you."

"Please, I've dated enough nuts in the past."

Laughter, low and throaty, flew from Karen's lips. "Okay, I

have an idea. Let's take stock of all the events." She lifted her index finger, poised to keep count of her points of emphasis. "One. He held your hand. Two. He asked you to a movie."

"Actually, I asked him. He just sort of reminded me."

"Same thing. That shows he wanted to extend his time with you. Three. Even after the movie, he kept you out until midnight, then the man—who is no spring chicken from what you've told me—"

"Hey, he's not *that* old."

"He's not that young, either, and he still woke up early so he could spend another hour and a half sitting next to you. Poor guy. While you slept in and went to a late service, he was fighting sleep and is probably snoozing right now in his recliner while the football game plays on without him."

The image brought a twitch to Esther's lips.

"Oh, wow. This is serious." Karen's awe-filled voice broke through with crashing reality.

"Serious? I've known the man a couple of days!"

"I knew the first time I saw Brian that he was the man for me."

"You were only kids."

"Maybe so, but the moment he helped me off the ground after our bikes collided, I saw what he would be. To me, he was everything he is today. Steady, reliable, a wonderful husband and father, and the sexiest man alive."

Esther grinned and glanced toward the barbeque pit at the other end of the yard. The "sexiest man alive" rubbed his hand over his balding head as he nodded at something Dad was saying. His T-shirt hung large and long to cover his middle-age spread, and his legs below his knee-length shorts could cause an accident on the highway if the sun shone on them just right.

Karen's chuckle indicated she knew exactly what Esther

was thinking. "He's mine. White legs and all, and I wouldn't trade that man for anything in the world."

"You're blessed, Karen. And I'm so glad you don't take it for granted."

Reaching out, Karen took her hand and squeezed. "You know, God had other plans for you all these years. But He knows how badly you want a family. Maybe Tom's entered your life for such a time as this, just like the Esther in the Bible."

Esther turned her attention to the three children who had tired of the hose and were now batting a volleyball back and forth over the net. Would this sort of life ever be possible for her? Or was it too late?

ﾞﾞ

"I think you should call her tonight, Dad. How's she going to know you're interested if you don't tell her?"

Tom looked at his daughter's face, slightly puffy from her pregnancy, and grinned. "If she doesn't know I'm interested after yesterday, then she's thicker headed than I am."

"You can't assume where matters of the heart are concerned. You have to let women know you're still interested."

"Still?"

"Yeah."

"Are we talking about you and Trevor or Esther and me?"

Her cheeks pinkened. "I mean, a girl can't read a man's mind. Trevor hasn't told me he loves me in days. I'm starting to think he finds me repulsive now that I'm so fat."

His heart clenched for her. She was far from fat or even chubby, and her husband adored her. Anyone within a hundred miles could see the love and adoration shooting from him whenever she walked into the room. But maybe he wasn't communicating it.

"All right, I'll call Esther, if you'll talk to Trevor."

Tears sprang to her eyes, and she didn't try to deny her

feelings of rejection. She nodded and offered a tremulous smile. "Deal."

Tom opened his arms, and she walked into them. Resting his chin on her silky hair, Tom felt a lump rise to his throat and his own eyes misted. Where had the years gone? It seemed like just yesterday, they were welcoming Ashley into the world, changing diapers, fixing bottles. And now she was about to do all those things for her own baby.

The thought of being a grandparent had gradually grown on him, and now he looked forward to bouncing the tyke on his knee and sending him home at the end of the day. The best of both worlds without the constant responsibility. At least Ashley and Trevor would have the benefit of a partner to lessen the load of parenting—not that he resented a single minute of the time he'd spent raising his three children. But it hadn't been easy. And he'd failed in so many ways.

Ashley pulled away from his embrace with a sheepish grin. Tom reached across to the counter and presented her with a box of tissues. "Thanks," she sniffed, taking two from the box. "I'm being silly, I know. These hormones make me nuts."

Tom took her shoulders and pulled her in so he could press a kiss to her forehead. "I know about those. Your mother cried at the drop of a hat when she was expecting you kids. But let me reassure you from a man's perspective. There's nothing more beautiful to a man than the woman he loves growing with his child. Unless it's the woman he loves holding his child in her arms. But you need to go and tell the father-to-be that you need to hear that he loves you." His eyes twinkled. "You'll probably hear it more than you want to from here on out."

"Ha! Not possible. Thank you, Daddy." Tiptoeing, she kissed his cheek. "I'm going to talk to Trevor right now. Go call Esther."

Tom smiled after his daughter as she waddled into the living room and touched her husband's arm. Trevor looked from the Cowboys' game to her face. He covered her hand with his and his expression softened with love.

Tom sent a grateful prayer to heaven. How many men would have asked her to wait until after the game—or at least until after the current play? God had blessed his daughter with a man who would love her first after God. Tom couldn't have picked a better man to take over the protection of his daughter.

He glanced at the phone, and his pulse quickened at the thought of what awaited him should he pick up the receiver and dial Esther's number. He'd been a little worried when he didn't see her at the early service. Lukewarm faith wasn't an attractive quality in a prospective wife for him. He wanted someone with a strong relationship with God. Ashley's news that Esther had attended the second service had delighted him.

Glad for the excuse of his promise to Ashley, Tom crossed to the phone and lifted the cordless off the charger. He pulled out the business card she'd offered him with her handwritten home number.

At the third ring, she answered.

"Esther?"

"Yes?" The confusion in her tone didn't bode well for his ego.

"It's Tom."

"Hi, Tom. It's nice to hear from you."

Okay. So far so good. She could have said, "Tom who?"

"Ashley said I should. . ." He winced. Bad, bad way to start. "I mean, well, she didn't make me. . ." Oh boy. He gathered a deep breath. "Do you want to go out again?"

"Are you sure you do?" Her tone was guarded, and Tom couldn't really blame her.

"Look, I'm sorry. I started off all wrong. I don't blame you if you say no."

"Wait. Do you want me to turn you down?"

"Well, no. It wouldn't have made any sense to ask you out if I didn't want to go out with you."

She gave a charming half laugh. "All right. Then my answer's yes."

"Yes?"

"Yes. Look, are you sure?"

Dropping into a kitchen chair, Tom released a sigh. "I'm really bad at this. Forgive me. How about if I stop trying to be smooth and just tell you the truth?"

"That sounds like a good idea."

"I enjoyed myself yesterday more than I thought I ever would again with a woman. I'm thinking long-term thoughts, and it has me a little rattled. But not scared. So you need to know up front that I'm not playing games. I have a feeling this could develop into something permanent and that's what I'd like to explore."

"I–I see. . . ."

Tom groaned inwardly. What kind of an idiot was he? *Sayonara, baby. There's no way she's going to agree to a date now.*

"Are you still there, Esther?"

"Yes. I'm just trying to digest the information. That's a lot to put on a girl so soon."

"You're right. But neither of us are children. We're mature. . . grown-ups."

He cringed. Why not just call her old? "I didn't mean—"

She laughed. "I knew what you meant. But your honesty is refreshing. And I agree with you. This could very well lead to something long term. And I'm willing to test it and see if maybe God has a plan in bringing us together."

His heart jumped. "How about dinner tomorrow night? I

know a steak house just off the interstate about twenty miles from town that has the best T-bone I've ever had."

"Oh, Tom. I'm afraid my week is full. One of my other clients is being audited, and I'll be working night and day."

"When will you be available?"

"Friday evening?"

Irritated at the thought of the long week ahead, Tom fought the urge not to press for an earlier date.

"All right. Friday. Can I pick you up at your house this time? Or is it still too soon? If you're more comfortable meeting there. . ."

"No. Not at all. Pick me up at seven." She gave him her home address.

Tom's face split into a cheesy grin even though no one was around to see it. No one had to tell him it was cheesy; he could feel it. He felt like a sixteen year old making his first date.

"Do you have an e-mail address, Tom? It'll be hard to catch me by phone this week."

"Uh. . .yeah. Wood4U." He gave her the ISP server name ending with dot com but didn't mention he'd never actually used it.

She laughed. "Catchy. Okay. I'll e-mail you this week and confirm our plans."

"Sounds good. I look forward to hearing from you."

"Bye, Tom, and thanks for being so open about your expectations. I'm so tired of the dating game."

The phone clicked before he could respond, but his heart lifted, and he felt like clicking his heels together. He headed into the living room, where Chris sprawled on the sofa watching the game in solitude.

Tom ruffled the teen's hair. "Chris! Come show me how to get into the e-mail program!"

Monday 9:30 a.m.

Dear Tom,
    Just a quick note to thank you for inviting me to the picnic on Saturday. I, too, had the best time that I can remember having in a very long time. I'm looking forward to seeing you again on Friday.

                                                    Esther

Monday 10:45 a.m.

Dear Esther,
    I'm glad you had a good time. You certainly made my day, but then I guess I already told you that. Ashley says to tell you hello. She seems to like you a whole lot. That's important to me.

                                                      Tom

Tuesday noon

Dear Tom,
    Ashley is a special young woman. It's easy to see she has a good father. I like her, too, and, yes, it's important to me that your children accept me if things progress to a long-term relationship.

                                                    Esther

Wednesday 11:00 a.m.

Esther,
    I'm sorry I didn't return your E-mail yesterday. We had a hectic day at the office. Hectic in a good way. We got the contract for the new community building.
    I've been thinking about your comment from yesterday

where you said you want the kids to accept you. I have an idea. Would you consider having dinner at my house Friday night instead of going out? It would give you a chance to get to know everyone better.

Let me know.

Tom

Thursday 7:00 p.m.

Tom,

Congrats on getting the community center contract! I'm impressed. I, too, have had a hectic week and I'll be glad to see it end. Dinner at your house sounds lovely. What time should I arrive?

Esther

Friday 10:00 a.m.

Esther,

I'm pleased you have agreed to dinner with the kids. I'd warn you about Minnie and Chris, but you've already met them, so I'm sure you know what you're getting yourself into. I've already threatened Chris if he asks you to be his new mommy again. That kid is making my hair gray. LOL (Ashley said that's how you say "laughing out loud" in e-mail code).

I'm looking forward to seeing you around seven. I'm knocking off work a bit early to fire up the grill. We'll have those steaks after all. Only I'll be making them for you instead of ordering them.

Tom

Tom pressed SEND on the e-mail program and sat back in his office chair, smiling. Finally, the endless week was over, and he'd get to see the woman whose face had sweetened his dreams and distracted his waking hours all week.

"Daddy!" Ashley's weak voice drifted from the doorway of his office. Tom glanced up. His daughter's face was drained of color. She held onto the doorframe. "Daddy," she said again. "My head hurts so bad."

Tom shot from his seat and reached her just in time to catch her before she fainted. He picked her up and carried her to the office couch. The blood rushed to his head at the sight of his girl, unconscious and unresponsive. In a state of panic, he grabbed the phone and punched in 9-1-1.

four

Caught in traffic, Esther glanced at the clock above the radio. *Seven-fifteen*. Four cars ahead of her, the light stayed red while the cross traffic sped through the intersection. Esther took the opportunity to smooth on face powder, a touch of blush, and lipstick.

She scowled at her reflection. This quickie makeup job was not how she'd envisioned her appearance for this evening. But an insistent client had barged in just before closing and demanded to see his books. No amount of reasoning could talk him out of it. Now, she was frazzled, late, and forced to wear the same outfit she'd had on since six-thirty this morning.

The light changed from red to green. Esther tossed the cosmetics onto the passenger seat and prepared to accelerate. She gave a frustrated sigh as the car in front of her sat unmoving. Clenching her fists, she fought for control. *Don't honk, Esther. Under any circumstances. There will be no honking.* The car behind her wasn't as resolved to good manners and blasted its horn. Esther cringed as the driver in front of her glared through the rearview mirror before gunning the motor. When she finally parked alongside the curb in front of Tom's two-story frame home, she felt unkempt, unprepared, and unattractive. Still, her heart leapt at the thought of seeing him again.

After another quick check in the mirror—and a responding grimace—she got out of the car and headed up the walk to the front door. She rang the doorbell on the "Waltonesque"-looking home. Minnie answered.

"Yeah?"

"Uh, I'm. . ."

"Oh, yeah. Dad's new girlfriend."

A flush of embarrassment burned her cheeks. She forced herself to remain in control. "I wouldn't exactly call myself his girlfriend after one date and a few e-mails."

Minnie gave her a knowing lift of brow. "So what brings you by? Eileen, was it?"

Esther gave a tight smile. "Esther." *As if you didn't know!* "Your dad invited me to dinner. Is he around?"

"That's weird."

"What is?" As far as she was concerned, it was anyone's prerogative to walk around with a boulder-sized chip on their shoulder if they chose to do so—as long as they didn't infect her atmosphere with the sour attitude.

"Dad isn't here. As a matter of fact, he left a message on the machine. Something about not making it home for dinner and we should grab something ourselves."

Esther blinked at the girl, not sure she'd heard her right. "Your dad isn't coming home for supper? Did he mention me at all?"

Minnie shrugged and shook her head. "Sorry."

"I see." *What a creep!* He'd either forgotten or he'd totally blown her off. Neither excuse was acceptable as far as she was concerned. A combination of anger and bitter disappointment mingled inside her.

"Do you want to come in and wait?"

Hard-pressed to keep her tone civil, Esther backed away. "I don't think so. Thanks anyway. Nice to see you again, Minnie."

"Sure," the girl muttered.

Tears pricked Esther's eyes as she walked back to her car. How stupid was she, anyway? He'd been so convincing. She'd been sure he was on the level.

Stop crying! she commanded as one tear and then another slid down her cheeks. Oh, why at all times did the emotions have to fly out of control? More and more lately, tears flowed at the slightest pressure.

She yanked a tissue from her purse and looked in the rearview mirror—a futile attempt to fix her face before she drove through the nearest fast-food window. So much for a sit-down dinner with the family!

Just as she finished blowing her nose and cranked the engine, Tom's truck passed hers on the side of the road and pulled into the driveway. Too humiliated to face him, she slipped the car into gear and started to pull away.

"Esther! Wait!"

"Not on your life, Buddy." She accelerated, but the car went nowhere. A growl rumbled in her chest as the engine revved. She'd put the car in neutral! The delay was enough so that Tom reached her car and opened the door she'd forgotten to lock.

"Hey, where are you going?"

"Home. Apparently you forgot our arrangements for tonight."

Crouching next to her, he shook his head. "No, I didn't. I left a message on the machine. Minnie was supposed to call you and explain."

She sniffed and looked unbelieving at his convincingly innocent expression. Peering closer, she frowned. Lines of fatigue etched the corners of his eyes.

"Is everything all right? Minnie only told me you wouldn't be home for dinner. I assumed you'd forgotten."

"Come on inside. We can order pizza or something."

Relieved beyond words that he truly had a legitimate excuse, she pressed her hand against his cheek, rough from a day's worth of growth. "Oh, Tom. That isn't necessary. You've obviously had a tough day. We can have dinner another time."

His eyes filled with emotion, and he covered her hand with his and brought it to his lips. "Come on. Please."

Her heart nearly leapt from her chest as he stood and tugged gently, pulling her to her feet. "A—are you sure?" she asked. No power on earth could have forced her to resist his simple request.

The presence of such an appealing, strong, and capable man made her knees go weak. When he laced his fingers with hers, she thought she might die right there on the spot.

He smiled, showing attractive, well-kept teeth. "I'm glad you didn't get the message." Without releasing her, he walked her to the door. When she thought he might turn her loose, he tightened his grip and led her inside. The door opened into a spacious living room. Minnie sat Indian-style on the couch, a huge mug in one hand, a textbook spread open in front of her.

"Hi, Dad." Her brow rose as she spotted Esther. "Oh, you waited for him after all?"

"No, I. . ."

"I got home as she was leaving. Don't be rude. Now why didn't you give Esther the message?"

The girl frowned. "What message?"

"The one I left on the machine."

"All I heard was a message that you wouldn't be home for dinner."

Tom looked at his daughter, suspicion clouding his eyes. He crossed to the answering machine.

"You don't believe me?" she asked, her mouth dropping open. She jerked to her feet, snatched up her book, and brushed past him on the way to the stairs. "I'll be in my room when you want to apologize."

Apparently undaunted, Tom punched the PLAY button,

skipping through the tape until he found his message. "Minnie, I won't be able to make it home for dinner. Fix something for yourself or order in. I'm in a hurry, but I'll explain later. . . . Uh. . ." And the machine phased out.

Suddenly nervous to be witness to Tom's error, Esther looked at the floor, wishing she could slither away unnoticed. He still hadn't acknowledged his mistake. Curiosity got the better of her and she sneaked a glance at him.

"I guess the tape ran out of room." He gave her a sheepish grin. "So, no one said I was perfect. Do you mind waiting alone for a minute while I go up and apologize to Her Majesty, the Queen of the Wronged?"

Esther laughed, relief making her heart light again. Nothing showed a man's true character more than the way he reacted to his own mistakes. "Not a problem."

"Thank you. Make yourself at home. Humble pie doesn't take long to consume, so I should be back quickly."

Alone, she perused the spacious room. The living room phased into a lovely, yet simple dining area, and a double-door opening separated the kitchen from this room. Wooden floors, covered with two oval braided rugs, stretched over the entire area. A dusty bookcase boasted tons of books.

On an equally dusty curio cabinet in the corner closest to the front door, Esther spied an eight-by-ten-inch photograph of a much younger Tom and three much, much younger kids. She caught her breath at the image of a woman who could only be Tom's late wife. The woman smiled for the camera, a beautiful confident smile that said, "I'm happy, in love, and thrilled to be living this enchanted life."

Suddenly feeling like an intruder, Esther walked away from Tom's memories and settled onto the couch to wait. When the door flew open a couple of minutes later, she nearly jumped through the roof.

Chris stopped short at the sight of her, then his expression brightened with recognition. A smile, identical to his dad's, split his face. "Oh, hi. Esther, right?"

She stood, relieved he wasn't playing dumb like his sister had. "Right." She smiled and took his proffered hand. "Nice seeing you again."

"Same here. So where's Dad? He didn't leave you all alone, did he?"

"He went upstairs to talk to your sister."

Chris rolled his eyes. "What now?"

"I guess you'd better let him tell you that."

"He'd better let me tell him what?"

Esther turned toward the stairs, but she heard Tom's boots clomping before she saw his face. Minnie was right behind him, her eyes red rimmed as though she'd been crying.

"What happened this time?"

"Mind your own business," Minnie snapped.

"Whatever."

"Are you two forgetting we have company?"

"It's, um, okay. Really." Esther felt like an idiot. This was going to be one awkward dinner.

As if sensing her hesitance, Tom cupped her elbow. Warmth spread through her arm. She smiled.

"Who's up for pizza?" he asked.

"I ate at Shermon's after practice," Chris announced. "I think I'll hit the books. Angsley's giving his first test tomorrow."

"Good luck," Minnie said with a sniff. "Angsley's the worst."

Chris nodded. He turned to Esther. "It was nice to see you again. I'm sorry I can't stick around."

Esther's heart warmed to his generous spirit. She smiled. "I understand. Good luck on the test."

She was rewarded with a dazzling grin.

Tom turned to Minnie. "How about you? Pizza?"

"I'm low carbing."

"Oh, yeah. Well, what if we order you some hot wings?"

"Oh, sure. Eat pizza in front of me while I eat chicken wings."

Esther listened to the exchange and watched as Minnie reduced Tom to feeling like an unfit parent, all the while embarrassing him in front of a guest. Besides, she'd had enough. If she weren't a Christian and therefore required to walk in love, she'd be sorely tempted to tell off that girl. As it was, she felt it would be better to leave so Tom could deal with those in his house.

She placed her palm against his bicep. "Tom. I really need to be going home."

"Wait. What about that dinner I promised you?"

"Another time, maybe."

"Maybe?"

"Call me." She could feel his gaze upon her, burning a hole in her back while she walked to the couch and grabbed her purse. She headed for the door.

"Esther, wait a sec. I'll walk you to your car."

He cleared his throat loudly.

"Uh, Esther. Please don't leave because of me." Minnie stepped forward. "I'm just a grouch because of sugar withdrawal and. . .well, it doesn't matter. Suffice to say, I behaved badly. The truth is, I'm headed over to the hospital to see Ashley anyway. So you two order whatever you want."

"Ashley? Is she all right?" Esther turned the question to Tom.

He nodded. "I was getting around to telling you. She collapsed at work today. When I took her to the hospital, her blood pressure was through the roof. I've been worried about how puffy she's been, but just figured she was eating too much."

"Is she okay?"

"They're keeping her a few days to try to get her to lose the water retention and get her blood pressure down. If not, they might have to deliver the baby early."

"How early?"

"She's only six months along."

The worry lines creasing the edges of his eyes struck Esther's heart like a well-aimed arrow. "I'm sorry. I'll keep her in my prayers." And she meant it.

"Thank you. Are you sure you won't stay for dinner?"

"I'm sure. I think I better get home. I have a full day tomorrow."

"Saturday?"

"Yes. I'm painting my guest bedroom."

"I'd offer to help, but Ashley. . ."

"Oh, no. Don't think anything of it. Please tell her she's in my prayers."

"I will. Thank you."

Tom reached around her and opened the front door. Esther's heart sped up as he brushed against her. His gaze demanded hers, and she couldn't look away.

"Are you sure you can't stay?" he said, soft and filled with emotion.

Still battling with the disappointment associated with the crashing of the high hopes she'd ridden all week, she nodded.

Tom heaved a long sigh and nodded. "I understand."

"I'm sorry."

"Let me at least walk you to your car."

They walked in silence until they reached her car.

He snatched her hand and lifted it to his chest. "I wish you'd reconsider. My kids aren't all that bad once you get to know them."

"Oh, I didn't mean to imply—"

"You didn't." He gave her a sad smile. "But I can put two and two together."

"Tonight was pretty overwhelming."

"I understand." His jaw clenched. "I have a busy, full life with three kids. I can't apologize for that. But I understand if you don't want to see me."

"I'm not saying I don't want to see you. Just that I need a few days to make sure I can deal with everything a relationship with you would entail."

"I understand."

I understand. Every time she heard those words of resignation, she felt about two inches high. "Take a few days to deal with Ashley. And I'll pray about us."

He nodded and smiled. "Should I e-mail you?"

"Please do. Let me know how Ashley and the baby are doing."

He reached out and laced his fingers through her hair, cupping her head. Esther felt the world stop spinning, and she stood unmoving, though her heart thundered like the hooves of a thousand horses.

"You have the softest hair."

Esther closed her eyes, relishing his touch and the sound of his husky, longing-filled voice. She knew all she'd have to do was lean forward and his lips would cover hers. With a shiver, she opened her eyes and stepped back.

Tom moved in closer until his face was inches above hers. "I'd like to kiss you."

She stared, unable to move. Unable to speak.

"But I won't. I know now isn't the right time."

A curious mix of disappointment and relief shifted through her. She glanced away.

"I'll let you go," he said softly.

Esther drove away, her mind whirling, trying to keep up

with the new emotions running amuck. How could she be feeling so strongly about this man after only a week?

And why was it the first man she'd had any significant feelings for came with a jumble of complications?

five

Tom clutched a stuffed elephant against his chest, praying fervently as his soft leather heels squeaked along the waxed hospital floor. Ashley's blood pressure had gone up and down over the last three days, necessitating a continued stay in the hospital. Tom had barely slept, barely eaten. And he'd worn a trail across his bedroom floor as he paced and prayed at all hours.

A petite, twenty-something day nurse with a carrot-orange bob and a smattering of cute freckles across her nose and cheeks came from Ashley's room and smiled, her eyes alight with recognition. "Hello, Mr. Pearson."

Tom nodded to her. Memories of his wife's final days slid through his mind. No one should have to stay long enough in a hospital that the staff knew family members by name.

The doctor had explained that Ashley's condition was extremely serious. Preeclampsia could easily escalate to seizures, organ failure, even death. Tom couldn't bear the thought of losing Ashley. The first few hours after calling 9-1-1 had been tense. And the last three days had been a jumble of highs and lows as her blood pressure stabilized and spiked, respectively.

Relief spread through him as he entered the room and saw his daughter sitting up in bed, laughing at a comedy/variety daytime show on the television. When she saw him, her countenance brightened even more. She clicked off the TV.

"Oh, boy, are you ever a sight for sore eyes. I'm dying for company."

Tom gave his girl an indulgent smile and set the stuffed elephant on the bed next to her.

"Oh, how cute! Thanks, Daddy."

Tom brushed a kiss to her cheek and dropped into the mauve, vinyl chair next to the bed. "How are you feeling?" The chair legs scraped the floor as he moved in closer.

"So much better." She held up both hands, wiggling her fingers. "See, the water retention is pretty much gone. My ankles are back to something resembling a human ankle."

"What's the doctor think?"

She sighed and leaned back. "Another day probably. My blood pressure has been good. They just want to make sure it stays near normal. When I go home, I'll have to stay on bed rest, though." A groan escaped her lips. "I don't know how I'm ever going to stay in bed that long."

"It's only for three months."

"Three months with only one of us bringing home a check?"

Tom's lips twitched. "You have a very generous boss."

Vehemently, Ashley shook her head. "No way. I'm not taking money from you."

"And I'm not going to let my daughter worry about having to pay the bills when she's about to give me a grandbaby."

He saw the softening in her expression as her eyes filled with tears. "We'll pay you back every penny."

Not a chance, little girl. "We won't talk any more about it for now. The important thing is that you stay healthy and get that baby here healthy."

"I know. You're right. Trevor is already laying down the law. 'No cleaning, no cooking—although I don't know what he expects us to eat—no laundry, no violent or scary movies or books." She laughed. "I have a keeper."

"And I thank God every day for sending you a man who will love you the way I loved your mother."

A reflective look crossed over her features, and when she looked at him, her eyes took on a serious glint. "Do you still miss Mama?"

Tom sent her a tender smile. "She'll always have a very special place in my heart."

"What about Esther? You haven't said much about her the last couple of days."

A jolt shot through his heart at the sound of Esther's name. By the rise of Ashley's silky blond eyebrows, Tom knew she'd noticed his reaction. He breathed a sigh. "She's taking a few days to sort through some of the issues associated with a relationship with me."

"Issues?" Her face clouded. "She'd be lucky to get you on your worst day."

Tom smiled at Ashley's defensive tone. And his heart went out to Esther for a split second. She'd never known the joy of holding her own newborn child. First day of school, first dance, first child's wedding. First grandchild. She'd never known the joys and worries of parenthood.

Sympathy clutched his chest, and he rose to Esther's defense. "She's never been married. Never had kids. My life is a lot more complicated than a single working woman's."

Ashley stretched out, wiggling her toes beneath the light covers. "I don't know, Dad. She doesn't seem that petty to me. I think she just got a little freaked."

"Oh? And how would you know?"

She sent him a sheepish smile. "All right, so I wasn't exactly clueless about the other night. Minnie spilled the whole thing."

Tom scowled, reliving the entire incident.

"Minnie feels bad, you know. She was having a tough day." Ashley's tone pleaded for Tom not to hold a grudge. As if he could hold a grudge against one of his children, even one who constantly challenged him like Minnie tended to do.

"Yeah, no kidding. Who wasn't having it rough that day?"

"Anyway, I think Esther's just scared. If I were you, I'd definitely give her a call."

"I've e-mailed her a couple of times."

"Did she write back?"

Remembering the short answers, Tom sighed. "Yeah, if you can call it that."

"Okay. Listen. You need to take matters in hand or she's going to do something you'll both regret."

"What would you have me do?" He gave her a wry grin. "Toss her over my shoulder and carry her to Vegas for a wedding?"

"Not a bad idea," she shot back, her plump cheeks pushing out farther, giving her a Shirley Temple adorableness he hadn't seen since she'd lost her baby fat around seventh grade. "But I was thinking more along the lines of a token of your affection. Something that speaks of a desire to raise the stakes of the relationship."

"Oh, good idea, Ash. Especially when she's running away. I'd say the last thing she wants is to raise the stakes."

"Maybe she just wants you to give her a good reason to see that being with you is worth complicating her life for."

"You mean chase after her?" Taken aback, Tom considered the possibility. "I've been giving her time to think."

"Oooh, bad choice."

"Hey, it's called respect."

"Send her flowers, Dad." She gave him a sassy grin. "I'd respect a dozen roses."

He leaned forward and chucked her chin. "I'll think about it."

Tom stayed until Ashley dozed. Taking care, he stood and bent over his daughter—the woman he would forever see as his little girl. She moaned and shifted as he kissed her head.

He left the room, his mind spinning with ideas. The image of Esther invaded his senses; her wholesome beauty and easy smile, the sweetness of her perfume, silkiness of her hair, the melodic sound of her laughter floating on the breeze. A longing ache pressed his chest like a cement block. Should he send the flowers or leave Esther alone as she'd asked?

As he walked past the hospital gift shop, baskets of pink and white carnations, plants, and single-flowered vases called to him. He resisted the overpriced shop, but when he slid under the steering wheel of his truck, he turned toward the closest florist.

ᴀ

With a half growl, half sigh, Esther clicked out of her e-mail program. Not one word from him. She'd been an obsessive e-mail-checking idiot all day at the office. Now, curled up with her laptop, trying to finish up some work at home, she couldn't stay offline. The e-mail program called to her with the taunting fear that if she stayed offline for more than two minutes, she'd miss a message from Tom.

"Stop being ridiculous," she admonished aloud.

It was her own fault. You don't push a guy away, barely answer his e-mails, and expect him to stay interested.

A frown played at her brow as she recalled their last meeting. He'd been so worried about Ashley. What if she'd taken a turn for the worse? Could that be the reason for his silence since yesterday afternoon? Esther stared at the computer screen, debating whether she should e-mail, call, or leave it alone. She reached for her cell phone just as the doorbell chimed, nearly sending her through the roof.

While her heart returned to a rhythmic beat, she cast a disparaging glance at her sloppy sweats and oversized Goofy T-shirt—her at-home uniform and not exactly the outfit she wanted to wear to open the door for anyone other than the pizza guy. And since she was eating chocolate chip cookies and vanilla ice cream for dinner, she knew it wasn't him.

She reached for the doorknob, then stopped as Karen's voice screamed through her head. *Never, ever answer the door without looking out the peephole. That's what it's there for!*

Obeying the voice in her head, she peeked out and frowned, her brain trying to process what she was seeing. Then realization dawned and she smiled widely. A bouquet of flowers hid the bearer of the gift, but she could imagine who was standing behind the blooms. Breathlessly, she opened the door.

"Hi!" The smile died on her lips as the wrong Pearson man held out pale pink roses.

Chris gave her a sheepish grin. "From Dad."

"I see." Disappointment that Tom wasn't the one standing on her doorstep mingled with a sense of glee that he'd sent the flowers in the first place.

"Please come inside," she murmured, taking the offering.

"Thanks anyway, but I can't. I have a ton of homework."

"I understand. Thanks for being the delivery boy."

"You're welcome." Chris headed down the front steps. Then he turned back. "You know, Dad's a great guy. Worth a little hassle in my opinion." Without awaiting an answer, he jogged to his old, yellow Toyota and chugged away.

Burying her face in the fragrant blooms, Esther felt a surge of affection rising in her. If she was going to become involved in a ready-made family, this one—Minnie notwithstanding—wasn't a bad choice. Surely, Chris and Ashley would make up for their sister's hatefulness. On the other hand, there was a lot to be said for an easy, uncomplicated life—one where no college-age girls infected her space with their spite, where she wasn't forced to share the attention of the man in her life. She chewed her lip and frowned. Of course, there was no man in her life at the moment, nor had there been for quite some time. Was being so picky worth the payoff of loneliness?

She stepped inside and leaned back against the closed door. The phone rang and she ran to snatch it up. Her heart leapt when Tom's low voice filtered through the line. "Hi."

Swallowing hard, Esther could hardly breathe. "Hello, Tom."

"Chris just called. He said he made my delivery."

"Yes, he did. They're lovely. Thank you." Her knuckles grew white as she clutched the phone tightly, at a loss for anything else to say.

Obviously plagued by the same loss, Tom cleared his throat but didn't speak.

Esther took the initiative and baled them both out of the awkward silence. "So, how's Ashley?"

"Better, thank God. She'll be going home tomorrow."

"I'm so glad, Tom. I've been praying for her."

"We appreciate it. The doctor has put her on a strict no-salt diet, and he wants to see her every week. She's not crazy about being on bed rest for three months, but she's willing to do it for the baby's sake."

"I'm sure any price is worth it to deliver a healthy baby." She closed her eyes, and for a second she could almost hear the deafening sound of her biological clock ticking. Her mind conjured the image of herself, big bellied and swollen ankled. Oh, how it would be worth every second, every pound.

"So, Esther. I was wondering if you'd be interested in having dinner with us tomorrow night? We're having a welcome-home dinner for Ashley, at her house of course, so she can stay on the couch with her feet up."

On the verge of saying yes, Esther stopped short of doing just that as a twinge of nerves hit her full in the gut. The memory of Minnie's animosity and the frazzled state of Tom's home sent her scrambling for an excuse. Tom might be a great guy, but he came with complications she wasn't sure she could deal with.

"I'm afraid. . ." She cleared her throat, the pause long enough for her to consider what she'd just said. She really *was* afraid. Ice-cold feet—that's all this was? She almost laughed. Never once had she allowed fear to hold her back from something she really wanted. So why was she running like a frightened rabbit at the thought of a lovely relationship with the man who could very well be the one she'd dreamed of her entire life? Still, she needed to sort things through. Talk it over with Karen.

"I'd better not this time, Tom."

"I understand." The disappointment in his tone filled Esther with regret. But she needed time to think things through. She had never been faced with falling for a guy who had kids. She'd stayed pretty much off the market, convincing herself she was happily single. Married to her job.

"I'm sorry, Tom."

"It's okay. I really do understand. I'll talk to you later."

"Bye."

Esther's lip trembled as she hung up the phone. Without taking time to think about it, she punched in Karen's number. When her sister answered, Esther barely gave her a chance to say hello before she launched into her tale of woe.

"Esther! This guy sounds like everything you've always dreamed of."

"I know, but things were so chaotic the other night. And Minnie was so hateful."

"Look, relationships have their ups and downs. Smooth sailing isn't even possible. I might not have the stepchildren issue to deal with, but we have plenty of struggles of our own. It sounds to me like Tom is worth a little hassle in order to find love."

Esther gave a short laugh. "That's what Chris said."

"Chris?"

"His son."

"So you see. . .even the guy's kids think you two have something worth pursuing."

"I suppose you're right."

"Of course I am. Now how about giving him a call?"

"I might."

"Esther!"

"I have to go. Thanks for lending the ear."

"My pleasure. Call him."

Esther sat back on the sofa and picked up her laptop. After a futile thirty minutes of pretending to crunch numbers, she gave up and reached for the phone.

Gathering a deep breath, she punched in Tom's number. She let it ring until the machine picked up, then she replaced the receiver without leaving a message.

The memory of his hurt tone struck her anew. Had she blown it? Suddenly nothing was more important than hearing his voice. She wasn't above begging if she had to in order to let him know she was ready to push past her fear and pursue a relationship with him.

After a quick search through her address book, she found his cell number and dialed. She released a relieved breath when he answered.

"Hi," she said, her heart pounding against her chest.

"I'm surprised to hear from you."

"Happy surprised?"

He chuckled. "To tell you the truth, yes. But I can't talk right now. I'm in my car and just got to where I'm going."

Swallowing her disappointment, Esther nodded, though

there was no one in the room to see her. "No problem. I'll try to call you later."

"All right."

The doorbell chimed as she pressed the button to disconnect. "What is this?" Esther muttered. This was the most action her door had gotten in one day for as long as she could remember. Without bothering to check the peephole, she flung open the door.

Tom's smiling face greeted her. "Hi," he said around an arrangement of carnations. "Roses didn't work, so I thought you might prefer these."

Esther laughed. "You mean you were outside *my* house?"

He nodded. "Can I come in?" His demeanor took on a seriousness that caused her heart to lurch.

Opening the door wider, she stepped aside. "Of course."

Once inside, he held out the flowers. "These are for you." His gaze sought hers with such questioning, she stepped back to escape the intensity of his ocean-blue eyes.

"Th–thank you. I'll find a vase to put these in." Grateful for the excuse to escape the tidal wave of emotion rushing over her, Esther snatched the carnations and fairly flew to the kitchen. Her hands shook as she filled a vase with water. She didn't dare handle anything sharp, so she left the stems uncut.

Fighting for composure, she captured a quick glance at herself in the mirror above the sink. Horror filled her at the sight. Her hair had fallen from the barrette she'd used to pull it back at six-thirty this morning. The Goofy shirt and sweats didn't look any better than they had earlier, and her makeup had long since worn off. All but the black smears under her eyes where she'd rubbed away the threat of tears earlier. She'd be lucky if Tom hadn't taken the opportunity to run off while she was in the kitchen.

After finger combing her hair and wiping away the black smudges with a paper towel, she gathered a deep breath and pushed back through the kitchen door. The sight of him made her knees go weak. A light blue denim shirt rolled up at the sleeves revealed deeply tanned, muscular forearms. For a forty-five-year-old man, he looked pretty good in a pair of Levis and cowboy boots. His slow smile nearly caused her to have a heart attack.

"Have trouble finding a vase?"

"No. Just trying to fix myself up a bit before I came back." She gave him a sheepish smile. "It's been a long day. Do you have time to sit?"

He nodded. "Thank you."

He sat on the sofa, leaving Esther with a dilemma. If he'd sat in the chair, she could have taken a seat on the couch without a problem. But now she had to decide whether to sit next to him on the couch and possibly give him the wrong idea or sit in the chair and appear aloof, standoffish, scared silly, or all of the above.

A chuckle rumbled his chest, and he patted the cushion next to him. "Let's talk about why you decided to call me after turning down dinner tomorrow night."

Heat rose to her cheeks as she sat next to him. Shoulder to shoulder with Tom, feeling the warmth radiating from him, she had trouble forming a sentence.

Tom patted her hand. "Let me tell you why I came over with flowers after you shot me down an hour ago."

"I didn't exactly shoot you down," she replied wryly.

"That's a matter of opinion." He turned and faced her, his knee brushing against hers. Reaching out, he took a strand of hair between his thumb and forefinger.

Esther shivered at the intimate gesture. He peered closer.

"I think we have something promising between us. No

woman has held my interest since my wife died, and I think this is worth pursuing."

"I agree," Esther said quietly, keeping her gaze fixed on his.

Surprise lit his eyes. "You do?"

She nodded.

"I was all set to argue my case."

"Your case?" Amusement lit inside of Esther. "Am I a judge?"

"You're definitely the one deciding the future of this relationship."

She nudged him with her elbow and sent him a saucy grin. "Would dating me be a jail sentence?"

He took her hand, its warmth filling her with all sorts of heady sensations. "No. If you give our relationship a chance, you'll be setting me free."

What was a girl to say to that? The laughter died on her lips. Twice, she tried and failed to respond.

Tom smiled. "So why were you calling me?"

Finding her voice, she turned her hand in his and laced their fingers. "I wanted to tell you that if you're still willing, I'd like to explore where this attraction between us might lead."

"Then I think we're on the same page."

An overwhelming sense of relief flooded her. "I think we are."

"I'd give anything to kiss you right now," Tom said, his voice low and husky with promise.

And she'd give anything to make that happen. Despite the sirens going off in her head, she closed her eyes and welcomed a kiss, imagining the feel of his warm lips on hers. How many years had it been since a man had held her in his arms?

Instead of the expected kiss, she felt Tom stand, pulling her to her feet with him. Her eyes popped open and she felt the blush rising to her cheeks.

"We have to get out of here. I'm just a man, Esther, and I haven't dealt with feelings like this in many years."

"Of course, I'm sorry."

"Don't be. You're a desirable woman and I'm developing feelings for you faster than I would have thought possible. I just don't want to do anything to offend you or compromise you in any way."

Well, that did it. In an instant, Esther left her long-term romance with her job and transferred her affections to Tom, all the while imagining white lace and promises.

"Let me change into something more presentable, and we can go get some coffee."

She gathered a shaky breath as she headed for the bedroom, feeling his eyes on her as she went. There was no turning back now. She'd opened her heart to this man in a matter of minutes.

A smile tipped the corners of her lips and confidence rose with each step. After all these years alone, just when she thought the romance train had passed her by, the Master Conductor had sent her the man of her dreams. The rest she'd deal with as she had to. For now, she was going to enjoy holding hands and seeing that wonderful smile flashed in her direction.

Oh, God. You are so good.

six

The grill sizzled as Tom slapped another burger onto the already overloaded rack.

"Whose idea was it to invite twenty college-age kids and their appetites to a barbeque?" he asked with a lighthearted growl.

Esther, who had pitched in like a real trooper to make Minnie's twenty-first birthday bash a rousing success, patted his arm as she walked by. She set a bowl of freshly made potato salad on the picnic table and grinned. "You're a great dad, do you know that? Minnie's birthday is a big hit because of your efforts."

The mild irritation sifted from his chest, and he returned her smile. "Sometimes I think Minnie got the raw end of the deal where I'm concerned. Ashley is my first child and Chris my only boy. I don't always know how to relate to Minnie."

Esther touched his arm, sending warmth through his bicep as her hand lingered. "You'll figure it out."

He covered the grill and set the spatula on the side table. "I'm afraid it might be too late. She resents almost everything I do or say."

"It's never too late to mend relationships." Esther's eyes beckoned him to believe in her words. Tom shook his head, marveling at her beauty—skin that invited caresses, hair that caught the sun in shimmers of golden light, eyes a man could drown in. Thoughts of her filled every waking moment and invaded his dreams.

A pretty blush crept to her cheeks. "Why are you staring?"

He reached out and snagged her about the waist, pulling

her close. "If I *weren't* staring, you'd have the right to ask me why. But I don't need a reason to look at you. You're beautiful. I can't keep my eyes off of you."

A smile curved her full lips, captivating Tom. They'd been dating for two months, and so far, he'd only given her a few cursory kisses on the cheek when he dropped her off, but he'd resisted long enough. He was going to kiss her. Now. And they'd just have to learn to resist anything more than that. Her eyes widened as he dipped his head. She took in a breath of air, her lips parting slightly. She didn't protest as he took possession of her mouth. On the contrary, she melted against him as though she, too, had been waiting impatiently for this moment. When she wrapped her arms about his neck, he drew her closer and deepened his kiss.

A low wolf whistle followed by a deluge of catcalls brought him to his senses and he pulled away.

"Whoa, Mr. P, that was some kiss."

"Hey, who's watching the burgers?"

"Do you two need to be reminded you're to set an example for those of us who are young and impressionable?" Chris asked, a grin spread across his red face.

Tom glanced at Esther. Her gaze was averted to the deck floor.

"All right. Enough teasing."

"Way to go, Dad," Minnie hissed in full earshot of Esther. "Did you have to humiliate me on my birthday of all days?"

Chris stepped forward before Tom could reply. "You're just jealous because you're not the one getting kissed."

"Why don't you be quiet and mind your own business?" she shot back, her lip trembling. She brushed past and slammed through the sliding glass door.

Watching her go, Chris shrugged. "I was just kidding."

"Greg didn't show up?" Tom asked.

Chris shook his head. "No. And Mitch let it slip that Golden Boy is dating Danielle Kovak."

Tom saw the question in Esther's eyes.

"Minnie has had a crush on Greg for six years," he explained. "But he's never noticed her. At least not that way."

Sympathy slid across her face. "I understand how she feels. That's hard on a young woman."

Tom couldn't imagine Esther having that trouble in a million years, but he refrained from mentioning her looks again, lest she begin to worry that he was only attracted to her physically.

He turned his attention to the burgers. "Okay, these are done. Chris, gather the troops."

"I'll go see if I can find Minnie," Esther volunteered.

Surprise lifted Tom's brow. "You sure? She's not in a very good mood."

A smile played at her lips and she winked. "I think I can hold my own."

≈

Could she hold her own? Esther's stomach turned over as she found Minnie's bedroom door and knocked. The girl could quite possibly eat her alive.

"What?" Minnie's voice sounded muffled.

"It's Esther. The burgers are done."

"Fine. Tell my dad to save one for me. I'll eat after everyone is gone."

Realizing Minnie wasn't going to ask her in, Esther gathered a deep breath and turned the knob. "I'm coming in," she warned as she pushed open the door.

Minnie scrambled to sit up on her bed. Her cheeks were wet from tears and her chin-length dark blond hair clung to her face. "What do you think you're doing?" she demanded.

"I warned you." Esther's heart raced, but she returned Minnie's glare and took another step forward.

"I don't appreciate people walking into my room uninvited."

"Then you should have invited me in." She approached the bed. "May I?"

"Since you're not going to go away, you might as well."

Esther sat. "So the tears are over a guy, I take it?"

A scowl marred Minnie's face. "Listen, I don't need advice from someone like you."

Stung, Esther nodded, determined not to show her hurt. "Someone like me, Minnie? You mean a dried-up old maid?" It was on the tip of her tongue to tell the girl if she didn't sweeten her attitude, she might very well find herself forty years old and alone one day, too.

Minnie's bravado faltered before Esther's steady gaze. "That's not what I meant," she mumbled. Releasing a heavy sigh, she stared at her hands. "I mean someone who looks like you."

"I don't know what you mean."

Her lips twisted into a wry grin. "Do you think my dad is interested in your mind?"

"I hope he is," she said quietly.

"Well, all right. He likes you as a person, too. But I'm sure the looks were what attracted him in the first place."

Suddenly every word Tom had ever spoken about her looks flashed through her mind. Was their relationship only skin deep? Rousing herself from the troubling thoughts, she gave Minnie a stern glance.

"All right. Listen. You have twenty friends out there who love you. I understand how badly it hurts when you like someone, and he doesn't like you back, but don't just run away and pout. It makes you look bad."

Lines creased Minnie's brow and her eyes grew stormy. "I am not pouting, *Esther.*"

"Oh, really?"

"Yeah."

"I bet if I went outside and took a vote, odds would be in favor of you hiding up here moping over Greg Somebody."

"Big deal." Minnie flung the pillow across the bed, then she sat up. "You think?"

"What else would they think? Someone announces that the guy you have a crush on is dating someone, and you run inside and don't come back?"

Understanding registered in her blue eyes. She gave a grudging nod. "Yeah, I see your point."

"So, do you want to go back and join your party?"

A heavy sigh escaped. "I guess." She stood and glanced in the mirror over her dresser. "Fat with red splotches all over my face. I just can't win."

Esther's heart went out to her. "Go wash your face and use a touch of powder to cover your red nose."

Nodding, she walked into her bathroom, leaving the door open as she washed her face. She surveyed her appearance in the bathroom mirror and grimaced. "Too bad there's nothing to cover the bulges. Believe me, black isn't that slimming when you're my size."

Esther chuckled. "Believe me, it's not that slimming at any size. You are what you are."

Minnie came out of the bathroom holding a compact of face powder. "Well, what you are and what I am aren't exactly comparable."

Drawing a deep breath, Esther decided to take a chance on the new camaraderie Minnie seemed to be offering. "You know, I have to watch my weight, too."

Predictably, the girl sniffed. "I don't see how you can even compare us, Esther. I don't mean to be rude, but I'm twice your size."

"Yes, but if I don't watch what I eat for the most part and exercise regularly, I'll gain weight, too." She gathered a breath and decided to take the bull by the horns. "Would you be interested in coming to the gym with me?"

Was that a hopeful glint in Minnie's eyes? If it was, it was so fleeting that Esther would never be sure.

Minnie shook her head. "I don't like to sweat."

"Neither do I. But it's a necessary evil if I'm to stay healthy."

"I'll think about it. Let's head back to my party before the guys eat all the burgers." She gave a short laugh. "One good thing about Greg not showing up, at least I can eat without being self-conscious."

"You know, Minnie, you underestimate yourself. Have you ever considered dating Mitch? If I'm not mistaken, he's got a thing for you."

A laugh erupted from her. "Mitch? We've been best friends since kindergarten. He's like a brother to me."

"I see." But what Esther really saw was the love in Mitch's eyes every time he cast his glance at Minnie.

Minnie moved toward the door, then stopped. "I appreciate your coming up here. Dad never quite knows what to say."

"Well, what man understands the complexities that are woman?" Esther grinned and Minnie laughed.

"True."

Laughter around the picnic table died when they arrived back on the deck.

"Good grief," Minnie muttered under her breath. "What's their problem?"

Esther leaned in close and whispered, "Just smile and remember this is *your* party. You get to set the tone."

Minnie nodded. In an instant, she transformed herself from a sulking touch-me-not to a vivacious, outgoing young woman, sashaying to the table, grinning broadly. "Hey, did you leave a burger for me?"

Esther chuckled, watching the girl set a lighthearted

atmosphere. Tom's breath against her cheek diverted her attention and she smiled, turning to face him.

"How'd you manage it?" he asked.

"I don't know." She gave him a straightforward gaze. "I just talked to her without apologizing."

Tom's face reddened. "You think I coddle her too much?"

"I think maybe you feel so guilty about paying more attention to the other two children that you'll say anything to stay on Minnie's good side." She walked around him and grabbed a paper plate, then started loading a hamburger bun. She smiled over her shoulder. "Even if it means apologizing for something you didn't do."

"Are you trying to tell me how to raise my kids?" His responding grin belied the defensive words.

She nudged him with her elbow as she held onto her plate. "Never. I'm analyzing your parenting methods."

"Oh? And how do I stack up, Doctor?"

"Not bad. Not perfect. But certainly not awful."

"Not perfect, eh?"

Sending him a coquettish grin, Esther leaned in closer to him. "Nearly perfect."

"You're perfect," he said in a low voice.

Remembering Minnie's words earlier, Esther frowned. "Is that the only reason you like me?"

He drew back. "What do you mean?"

She shrugged and squirted ketchup onto her burger. She reached for onion slices, but remembering the earlier kiss, opted not to take the chance he might try again later and be offended by onion breath. "You love to tell me I'm beautiful. But you don't mention much else about me that you find. . .interesting."

Embarrassment caused her to falter under Tom's tender smile. She averted her gaze. He took her chin and raised her face to look her in the eye. "You think I'm only lusting after your beauty?"

Esther's cheeks flamed beneath his amused face, but she squared her shoulders and held her own. "Maybe."

"While it's certainly true that I find you attractive, I also love your humor, not to mention your intelligence—have you forgotten you take care of my finances?"

Seeing his point, Esther grinned.

Cupping her cheek in his palm, he continued, "I love the fact that you know God and serve Him with an honest heart. I love that you see beyond Minnie's surly attitude to the sweet girl beneath. I love that you are concerned for Ashley and laugh at Chris's nonsense. And, yes, I love to look at you because the wonderful, warm, funny person you are is all wrapped up in a gorgeous package. And if you have a problem with that, then you need to ask God why He made you that way and why He made me a man, because any man would enjoy looking at you."

With a short laugh, Esther pulled back and walked toward the deck furniture, away from the peering eyes of Minnie's guests. "They're not exactly beating down my door. Have you forgotten I'm an old maid?"

Tom chuckled and followed her, taking a seat next to her in the white-framed cushioned chair. "Lucky for me." He looked a little out of place on the pastel, flowery cushions. Esther wondered if it were time to replace the chairs and lounge, which had obviously seen better days—and had most likely been purchased under the watchful eye of his deceased wife.

Esther felt an instantaneous surge of jealousy for the unknown woman who had captured Tom's heart so many years ago and most likely still claimed a large part of it.

"How about coming back to the party?"

Tom's voice snapped her back to attention. "I'm sorry."

"You seem awfully far away."

There was no way she was going to admit to her train of thought, so she bit into her burger, instead. A huge bite— one that would keep her mouth occupied for awhile.

"Are you convinced yet that my affection is more than skin deep?" he asked.

Still chewing, she nodded, then swallowed hard. Tom handed her a can of Coke. "Here, take a drink before you try to talk."

She washed down the bite and gave him a sheepish grin. "I guess that's what's called biting off more than you can chew."

He groaned, rolling his eyes. "And did I mention your corny jokes are an endearing quality as well?"

Feeling a giggle coming on, she smothered it with another bite.

"Hey, we're going to play volleyball. Do you two want to join us, or are you too busy playing footsie?" Chris's teasing words invaded the conversation, but far from annoyance, Esther felt only thanks. This got her out of the hot seat with Tom.

Setting aside her half-eaten burger, she hopped to her feet. "I haven't played volleyball in ages."

"Okay," Chris announced to the group, "Esther's the hole. Send the ball to her for a guaranteed point."

"Hey!" Esther gave him a playful sock in the arm.

Chris grabbed her and lifted her into a bear hug. "You're a great sport," he said against her ear. "I'm glad Dad found you."

Tears pooled in her eyes. He set her on her feet and sent her a broad wink before sauntering away. Esther watched him go, a wistful sigh escaping her lips. She should have had a strapping son—someone to fix enormous meals for and worry over as he dated girls who were clearly not good enough for him.

Warmth enveloped her shoulders and she smiled at the

feel of Tom's hands. "You okay? He's a little exuberant."

"He's a great kid," she said. "I was just thinking how proud his mother would be." She heard the longing in her tone, but didn't care. Motherhood had never been a goal, not a real goal. Now, however. . .

Tom remained silent behind her, and Esther smiled, laying her cheek against the back of his hand, which still rested on her shoulder. She felt the gentle brush of his lips against her hair, and she closed her eyes, enjoying the intimate moment. And taking it for what it was—his assurance that he cared about her, that he understood her desire, but he wasn't ready to offer her the chance to become a mother.

The sun hung low in the sky, withholding some of its earlier warmth as evening approached and warning the volleyball players that they only had a few minutes of light in which to play their game. Fingers of pink and orange promised a beautiful sunset, and Esther breathed deeply of contentment.

Finally, her life seemed complete. She'd had her tough times, her lonely times. Surely, it was all gravy from here on out.

seven

The ringing telephone woke Tom from a deep sleep. Disoriented, he sat up straight, his heart beating a rapid cadence in his chest. He reached for the phone, glancing at the bedside clock. Three-o-six, in glowing red, marked the only light in the darkened room.

Who calls at three in the morning?

"Hello?"

Trevor's shaking voice filtered through the line.

Tom swung his legs over the side of the bed. "What's wrong?"

"A—Ashley had a bad, bad headache all day."

"That sounds like her blood pressure is up again. Did you call the doctor?"

"Yes, and she's doing better. . .but we should have known her headache meant her blood pressure was too high. We just didn't think."

"Okay, listen, Trev. Are you at the hospital?"

"Yes. They just took her to be examined."

"I'll be there in twenty minutes."

He hung up the phone and flew into action—praying as he dressed, praying as he pulled on his shoes, praying as he grabbed his keys and headed down the steps.

"Dad?"

Minnie's sleepy voice caught him just as he opened the door. "Hi, honey."

"Where are you going?"

"Ashley's in the hospital. Her blood pressure spiked again. That's all I know."

"Hang on. I'm coming with you. Chris! Get up. Ashley's in the hospital."

"I'll go warm up the car; if you're not out there in ten minutes, I'm leaving."

"Got it."

She made it in eight, Chris sprinting behind her carrying his gym shoes. They raced to the hospital in nearly zero traffic. By the time they reached labor and delivery, they were all three breathless. Trevor's face melted in relief when he saw them.

"They're going to induce labor. Her blood pressure is coming down, but it's still too high. The doctor is afraid that if he waits any longer, she could start having seizures."

"Why aren't they doing a C-section?" Minnie demanded.

"That's what the doctor wanted to do in the first place, but Ashley has her heart set on delivering the baby naturally."

"Is that safe?" Tom asked.

"Dr. Baker said they'll keep a close watch, and if she starts to have trouble, they'll have to do the C-section immediately."

"What did Ashley say to that?"

"You know Ashley." He gave a shaky grin. "She's trusting God that everything will work out the way she wants it to."

"Can we see her?"

"In a little while. They're getting the IV in and starting the drip to induce her labor."

Chris pulled out his cell phone and handed it to Tom. "Do you want to call Esther?"

Tom started to reach for the device, then pulled back. "No. This is a family matter. I don't want to bother her."

Minnie made a face. "Get real, Dad. You know she's going to be family soon. If you don't call her, you're going to make her feel like you don't trust her with our problems. But you can't use the cell phone in the hospital, spaz." She headed across the hall to a pay phone.

She punched in some numbers.

"You know her number by heart?"

"Yep." She held up her hand to silence him. "Esther?"

Tom and Chris looked on and listened to the one-sided conversation, deducing that Esther was immediately concerned, was coming to the hospital, and was glad Minnie had called.

She arrived within an hour, her face void of cosmetics, her hair pulled into a ponytail. She wore a pair of faded Levis, a St. Louis Rams sweatshirt, and a worn bomber jacket. And she was the best-looking thing he'd ever seen. He felt his tension release as warm air coming through the vents carried the scent of her sweet perfume.

A tender smile lifted the corners of her lips when she saw him, and she came to him, taking him into her arms. Tom buried his face in the soft curve of her neck. Minnie had been right. This woman was definitely going to be family. Soon.

"How is she?" Her warm breath against his ear sent a shudder through him. He pulled back and held her at arm's length.

"The doctor says her blood pressure is low enough for now. If it stays down, she can deliver naturally. Otherwise, they're going to have to do a C-section."

"Can we see her?"

"Yes. We can go in two at a time."

"Should I wait out here so your family can see her?"

Tenderness welled inside Tom's chest at the uncertainty in her voice, the wondering whether she was close enough to intrude upon a family situation. "Chris and Minnie are in the cafeteria getting breakfast. Come on. Ashley will want to see you."

They entered the room.

Ashley's face brightened at the sight of Esther. "I'm so glad you came."

Esther moved to Ashley's bedside and pushed a strand of hair from the girl's forehead. "How are things going, honey?"

"The contractions are getting stronger. I'm starting to feel them." She smiled. "I guess that's a good sign."

Tom frowned. Ashley hadn't told him she was in pain.

"So I've been told," Esther said wryly. "Can I get you anything to make you more comfortable?"

"Just knowing you all are here means so much to me."

The automatic blood pressure machine kicked in. Ashley made a face. "Ouch," she mouthed as the cuff tightened. When the numbers displayed her reading, worry lines etched the nurse's forehead. "That's pretty high. How's your head?"

Tears formed in Ashley's eyes. "It hurts."

"All right," the nurse said, her tone leaving no room for discussion. "Everyone out except the husband. I'm going to call the doctor."

Tom's heart picked up and his stomach began to churn. "What's going on?" he asked the nurse as they stepped into the hallway.

"Her blood pressure is spiking up, probably because of the pain from the contractions. I have to notify her doctor."

"Is she going to be okay?" He knew it was a ridiculous question, but he needed the reassurance. The nurse just gave him a look that clearly stated she wasn't making predictions.

Esther took his hand. "Come on. Let's go sit down. They'll let us know when they know something."

Tom allowed her to lead him to the waiting area. They sat on the cold vinyl chairs. He leaned forward and rested his elbows on his knees, forehead in his palms.

"She'll be all right, Tom."

"How do you know that?" he shot back. The quick hurt in Esther's eyes drilled into him like a bullet exploding in his chest. "I'm sorry."

"I understand," she said softly. But he could tell she didn't. He felt her withdraw emotionally, though physically she didn't move.

❧

Esther fought against the tears threatening to push their way to the surface. She truly did understand why Tom would snap like he did. He was wound so tightly with worry that Esther was surprised he hadn't yelled at the nurse. She didn't know what to say, so she remained silent and offered quiet support.

Tom took her hand. "I'm really sorry for snapping at you, sweetheart."

Esther drew in her breath at the endearment. She laid her cheek against his shoulder. "It's okay. Really."

"No. I shouldn't have barked at you. I'm just so worried." His voice trailed off. Esther raised her head to look at him, but remained silent, waiting for him to continue. After a few seconds, he did. "Being a parent is the greatest joy and the greatest pain in life. There's no way to describe the feeling of holding your baby for the first time. You spend their childhood trying to find a balance between protecting them and not holding too tightly. They get married and you think, 'Okay, now someone else will take care of her. I can stop worrying.' But I never stop wanting to take care of her. It's not that I don't feel like Trevor's a good husband. He is."

"She's been blessed to have two wonderful men looking after her."

Tom's eyes clouded with tears. "I've tried my best to make sure she's okay. But I realize how little power I really have. My daughter could be just down the hall having a seizure, and there's nothing I can do."

"Yes, there is. You can pray and trust the Lord's love for her. Remember, if you, as an earthly father, long to keep your daughter safe, how much more do you think her heavenly Father longs to see her through this situation she's going through?"

He nodded and squeezed her hand. "You're right. But knowing in my mind and releasing my daughter to God in my heart are two different things."

"It's called standing in faith. You are a man of faith. Search your heart and let God give you rest."

Chris and Minnie came into the waiting room. "Hey, they won't let us in to see Ashley," Chris said. "What's going on?"

Tom filled his children in on Ashley's condition.

Amid the barrage of questions, Trevor came into the waiting room, appearing shaken, his face drained of color.

Tom stood and went to his son-in-law. "How's Ashley?"

"They're prepping her for surgery right now. They're delivering the baby C-section. The doctor said if we wait, she might start having seizures." As though his legs were suddenly without strength, he sank into the nearest chair. "Oh, God. Please be with my wife and baby. Keep them safe."

Esther bowed her head with the rest of the group, and they followed Trevor's lead, each speaking aloud the prayer of his or her heart. For the next hour, they took turns pacing until the nurse arrived. A collective *whoosh* of relief left them as her smile registered.

"Mother and baby are doing well." She glanced at Trevor. "Congratulations, you have a six-pound, four-ounce son. He's doing great. We're going to keep him under the lamp for awhile and watch him since he's four weeks early. But he seems to be fine."

"And my wife?"

"Everything is returning to normal. That's the thing about preeclampsia. Once the baby is delivered, things usually straighten right up."

"When can I see them?" Trevor asked.

"The baby is on his way to the nursery right now, and you

can see him through the glass. You should be able to see your wife in a couple of hours."

Minnie grinned broadly. "Let's go see the baby!"

Esther had never heard her excited about anything before. She smiled and nodded. "I agree."

Tom hung back for a split second, then acquiesced. "I guess if we can't see Ashley for a couple of hours anyway, we might as well go get a look at my grandson."

Esther looped her arm with his, and they walked to the next hall.

"Look, there he is!"

"Is he okay?" Chris asked. "He looks a little sick."

Tom chuckled. "All babies look like that when they're first born. Don't worry, he'll fill out and perk up in no time."

Esther watched the look of adoration on his face as he looked at his grandson. An invisible hand of longing squeezed her heart. *Oh, Lord. I want one.*

Once she'd spoken the words in her heart, she realized how many years she'd been afraid to pray that prayer. Afraid to admit to such a desire when she had no prospects of marriage any time soon. Afraid the answer might be *no*. But as she peered through the glass at Ashley and Trevor's baby, tears streamed down her cheeks and hope sprang inside of her heart. Would she hold her own child one day?

Tom's arm slipped around her shoulders, and he pulled her close. "Isn't he something?" he whispered close to her ear.

"He sure is."

"Thank you for being here to share this moment with me, Esther. It means the world to me."

"To me, too." And perhaps, if God willed, they would be sharing the birth of their own child in a year or two. A smiled played on her lips as she closed her eyes and allowed herself to dream.

eight

If she hadn't been holding on, Esther would have slid right off the treadmill. The sight of Minnie standing in the doorway thrilled her beyond words. Dressed in black leggings and an oversized T-shirt, the girl looked ill at ease and shifted from one foot to the other. But she had pushed aside her angst and shown up.

A buff, twenty-something guy walked past, gave Minnie a once-over, and continued on as though she weren't worth his time. Indignation clutched at Esther and, if she hadn't thought it would mortify Minnie, she'd have run after the jerk and given him a good piece of her mind.

As it was, Minnie's expression crashed, and she looked as though she might turn and flee at any second. Esther quickly shut off the treadmill and grabbed her towel. Patting the sweat from her neck and brow, she hurried over to the girl.

"You came!"

Pink spots appeared on her cheeks, even as relief washed over her features. "Yeah," she mumbled. "I'm not sure it'll do any good, but thanks for inviting me."

"My pleasure. There's an available treadmill next to mine. Are you ready to walk or do you need to go to the locker room first?"

"I don't do women's locker rooms," she said, a wry grin playing at her lips. "I'll forever be scarred by my junior high and high school memories of skinny girls in their underwear."

Esther chuckled. "Me, too."

"Yeah, sure." Minnie gave her a look that plainly said she

didn't believe a word of it but appreciated Esther's attempt to make her feel more comfortable.

"Okay, then. Hang your keys on the little key holder there, and let's go get that heart pumping."

Rolling her eyes at her own attempt to motivate the girl, Esther shook her head. All she needed was a Minnie Mouse voice and she'd sound like Kiki, the gym's aerobics instructor.

Mindful of Minnie's lack of conditioning, Esther kept her own treadmill at a comparable speed, but increased her incline so she could still work at the proper level.

"So, how are things going?" she asked, resorting to the universal ice-breaking phrase. Not very original but, thankfully, it worked.

"Okay, I guess. I'm trying to wrap up a research paper that counts for half my semester grade in English."

"What's it on?"

"Obesity and the reasons girls get fat."

The plainspoken answer took Esther by surprise. But she also understood that Minnie was trying desperately to come to grips with her own physical condition. To find answers that might help her do something about her weight problems.

"And how's that going?"

Minnie gave a short laugh. "I'll tell you later when I can catch my breath."

After twenty minutes, Minnie was drenched in sweat and definitely looking ready for a little rest.

"How about going to the juice bar for a protein shake?" Esther suggested.

"Sounds good."

They grabbed towels and sat in a couple of stools at the counter. After ordering, Esther turned to Minnie. "So how is the paper coming along?"

Minnie shrugged. "Let's just say, I'm not entirely comfortable confronting myself. But I felt the Lord chose this topic for me. I mean, Ashley weighed less than I do when she went in to deliver her baby. Chris has eight percent body fat. Dad's thin and so was my mom. As far as I know, there's not one genetic reason I should be overweight. And yet. . ." She glanced down at her body, then shot her gaze to Esther.

"Have you come up with any answers?"

"Yep. It's all Dad's fault." She gave a saucy grin, but there was a hint of truth in her eyes.

Esther nearly choked on her sip of protein drink. Her eyes widened and she assessed Minnie's expression. The girl meant it. Knowing she had to tread carefully or risk undoing all the progress they'd made, she swallowed and focused on keeping her tone even. "How did you come to this conclusion?"

"Okay. It can't have escaped your notice that Ashley is Daddy's little princess. And Chris, well, he's the son. All men want that son, right?"

"I guess so."

"So that leaves me, not only the middle child, but the unnecessary one."

"Unnecessary? Oh, Minnie, that's a little dramatic, don't you think?"

"I don't mean I'm not loved. I know Dad loves me. But fathers need one princess to shower love on, and they need a boy to pass on the family name to—plus all that manly information like woodworking, fixing cars, and so forth."

"Okay, I can see your point somewhat. But I'm not sure where you're going with it. And I don't believe you're unnecessary by any stretch of the imagination."

"When I was growing up, Dad had a special thing he did with each of us so that we didn't feel our mother's loss so much. Ashley wanted ballet and gymnastics. So he took her to lessons, encouraged her, went to recitals, all that stuff. That was their special time together. He played ball with Chris and helped him make go-carts, taught him to shoot a gun. Guy stuff. You know what our special time together was?"

"What?"

"Once a week, we went to see a movie together. If nothing appropriate was playing, we'd go to a kid-friendly pizza place that had games and an arcade."

"That sounds like fun, Minnie. I don't understand your problem with it."

"Okay. What's the first thing you are aware of when you go into a theater?"

Perceiving how important this was to Minnie, Esther concentrated, wanting to get the right answer. She imagined herself walking into the theater, the smell of popcorn. . .ahh. . .

"Popcorn?"

"Bingo. I began to associate my time with Dad as a time to eat. That once-a-week outing with him was the best time in my life. All my happy childhood memories revolve around our times alone together. The happy smells and tastes of popcorn, nachos, pizza, Milk-Duds."

"I see your point, but I don't understand how you can fault your dad for wanting to spend time with you."

"I'm not really faulting him. It's just that his time with Ashley and Chris revolved around things they were interested in. He assumed I wasn't interested in anything, so he chose the easy way out with me and stuck with entertainment. The truth of the matter is that I wanted to take piano lessons. But he never asked me."

"Did you ever ask *him* for piano lessons?"

She shook her head. "I wasn't the type to ask for anything. But why didn't he notice that I always sat at mom's piano and tried to pick out songs by ear?"

"He's not a mind reader, honey. And I'm sure he treasured

those times with you and never thought about you not being satisfied."

"I know he did. He's a great dad. It's just tough not to be angry with him when I realize that I eat for comfort because food was the focus of my happy childhood memories." She grinned. "I'm also a movie junkie and I love computer games."

Esther couldn't resist the playful tone. She laughed, then grew serious. "You know, Minnie, I think you should talk this over with your dad. He's trying to understand your relationship, too."

Her brow rose. "He talks to you about me?"

"You're talking to me about him," Esther replied, appealing to her sense of reason in an effort to thwart the righteous indignation of betrayed privacy.

Thankfully, the ploy worked and understanding lit Minnie's face. "I see your point. So you really think I ought to talk to him?"

"I do. Keeping things hidden causes more problems than it's worth."

"You're probably right. Thanks, Esther."

Esther smiled and continued to smile throughout the day. Parenting obviously came easy to her. She was going to be a great mom.

❧

Esther finally had all she could take of Tom's staring at her from across the candlelit table. This was their first dinner together at her home and, so far, everything was perfect. His attention flattered her, and she normally enjoyed it, but not while she was chewing. She leaned forward. "Stop staring."

He cleared his throat and shifted in his chair. "Sorry."

Sending him an indulgent smile, she sipped her iced tea.

"How was your day?" he asked.

"Great. I got tons done at work. I'm gearing up for tax season, though. Right after Christmas, things really start hopping." Esther chewed the succulent prime rib and swallowed it down, debating whether or not she should bring up yesterday's conversation with Minnie. The girl had shown up again this morning, but had been tight-lipped, discouraging any kind of personal discussion.

She decided to approach the topic through a back door rather than bring Minnie up directly. "Minnie tells me Ashley gets to take the baby home tomorrow."

Tom beamed as he always did when anyone mentioned his little namesake. "We're having a welcome home dinner. You coming?"

"Is that an invitation?"

"Of course. Not that you need one."

"I'd be delighted, then."

"Good. Maybe you can help keep things from getting heavy."

"Heavy? How could there be anything but joy at Tommy's coming home party?"

He sighed. "Minnie is in another one of her moods."

"I noticed she seemed a little upset at the gym today."

"She came to the gym?"

"Yes. She's really serious about confronting her weight issues."

"Tell me about it. She's decided I'm solely to blame."

So the girl had spoken to him. Esther cringed. Maybe she shouldn't have encouraged Minnie in that direction.

"What'd she say?"

He repeated the things Minnie had confided to Esther the day before, only his eyes flashed with indignation. Guilty fear swept through Esther. She'd been the cause of this contention. Minnie probably never would have brought it up to Tom if Esther hadn't encouraged her to do so.

"Can you believe kids these days? It's not enough that we

sweat to provide for them, worry to death over their well-being, cry over their hurts." He shook his head. "Even the ones who admit they had a good parent find something to blame us for."

"I don't think she was blaming you, exactly, Tom." Feeling responsible for the entire misunderstanding, Esther felt she had to try to help patch things up between father and daughter.

Tom let out a short laugh. "Believe me. I'm to blame for every size above a six."

"Don't you think she's just trying to come to grips with her weight issues? It's difficult being a young woman her age as it is. But the added weight wreaks havoc with her self-esteem."

"I understand, but why not take matters into her hands and do something about it? I don't like being blamed just because she likes Twinkies."

Esther's defenses rose. "She is doing something about it. But some people need more than a physical response. Some people need to understand why things are as they are. For Minnie to lose the weight without understanding why she's heavy to begin with, she's likely to regain anything she loses."

"Is this our first argument?"

Taken aback by the abrupt change of subject, Esther had to take a second to readjust.

Tom smiled and Esther couldn't help but respond in kind.

"I guess I got a little carried away defending her," she admitted.

"And I guess I got a little carried away defending myself. Come on, I'll help you clean up."

Some of the joy had been sucked from the evening, and she wished she could go back to yesterday morning and mind her own business.

❧

Tom sensed her withdrawal but couldn't decide if he'd stepped over a line or not. He knew she was a little put out with him, but, for crying out loud, a man had a right to defend himself if someone accused him of being the cause of all her problems. He toweled a plate and set it in the cabinet and moved behind Esther. He slipped his arms around her waist and buried his face into the curve of her neck. She leaned her head back against his shoulder and released a soft sigh.

Tom swallowed hard, taking in the sweet scent of her perfume. "Look, I don't want us to be at odds," he murmured against her skin. "This is between my daughter and me. It doesn't have to be an issue with us."

She turned in his arms and laid her palms against his chest. "I have to tell you something. And you may not like it."

The worry on her face clutched at his heart. Mentally, he braced himself for what came next. "What's that?"

Averting her gaze from his eyes to her hands, she gathered a deep breath. "Okay, Minnie confided in me yesterday about all this. She told me about her research paper and about figuring out why she overeats."

"Yes?" Tom frowned, not entirely sure he liked where this was going.

"I—I actually thought she made a lot of sense."

That wasn't exactly what he wanted to hear. And she clearly wasn't finished.

"And I encouraged her to talk it over with you. I just assumed you'd be interested in hearing her out."

"And now you think I'm not only responsible for her condition, but an uncaring father as well?"

She caught his gaze and pulled back. "I didn't say anything about you being an uncaring father. Nothing could have been further from my mind."

"But you think I made her fat?"

"I don't believe it was your fault at all. You were being the best father you could have been to her. Even Minnie admits that you were great. But no one can predict how a child's experiences will affect them. Even the good experiences."

"So you're saying I handled Minnie all wrong?"

"That's not really my place to say. But I think sometimes we have to give ourselves the opportunity to see a situation through someone else's eyes, even if we know in our heart that we did the best we could."

He tightened his arms about her and pulled her closer. "You know what?"

A relieved smile curved her lips. "What?"

"I wish I'd had you around a long time ago." He pressed a quick kiss to her lips. "I might not've made so many mistakes."

"I wish you'd had me around a long time ago, too. But not to thwart inevitable mistakes." She raised her chin for a kiss. Delighted, Tom obliged. She smiled and continued, "It just seems like a waste of time for both of us to have been alone for all those years when we could have been sharing our lives."

Her eyes widened and she stepped back. "I didn't mean. . .I mean, I wasn't hinting."

Pulling her back into his arms, Tom muffled her rambling with a lingering kiss. He knew what she meant. Every moment they were together was precious time, and he regretted that he hadn't fired his former accountant and walked into Esther's office years ago. The soft warmth of her mouth beneath his invited a deeper kiss, but cognizant of the fact that they were alone in the house, he pulled away.

She sighed and laid her head against his chest. He stroked her silky hair. The words he'd been keeping in his heart for weeks suddenly spilled from his lips almost without warning. "I love you."

A soft gasp escaped her. She pulled back and caught his gaze. Her eyes shone. "You do?"

Taking her face in his hands, he returned her gaze, relieved to have the words finally out in the open. "I've only loved once in my life until now."

"I've never loved anyone before you."

Tom's heart thrilled at her admission. He pulled her close to him. "Say the words," he gently demanded.

"I love you." Her eyes misted; her lips trembled with the whispered words. Unable to speak, he lowered his head and covered her mouth with his. When he pulled away, they were both shaken and Tom knew he couldn't stay. They had planned a movie after dinner, but that was out of the question if they were to remain pure before the Lord.

"I'm going to go."

She nodded. "Yes, I think that's for the best."

"Don't walk me to the door."

Leaning against the counter, she watched him step back. Tom used every ounce of self-discipline he possessed to turn and walk through the kitchen door, grab his jacket, and leave.

In his car, he pulled his cell phone from his jacket pocket and dialed Ashley's number.

"Hi, honey, are you up for a little company?"

"Sure. I'm a bundle of energy waiting to bring Tommy home tomorrow."

"Okay, I'm calling Minnie and Chris. We'll be there in a little while."

He said good-bye and dialed home. "Minnie, get Chris and meet me over at Ashley's."

"Wait. Is Ashley okay?"

"She's fine."

"I thought you had a dinner date with Esther."

"I did. It ended early. Meet me over there. It's time for a family meeting."

nine

"Okay, I blew off an entire afternoon of work," Esther groused. "The least you can do is tell me where we're going. I don't see what couldn't wait until dinner tonight, anyway."

"The reason it couldn't wait," Tom said, with all the patience of Job, "is because I missed you." His heart-stopping grin nudged away some of her exasperation at being kept in the dark about where they were going. He'd come into the office thirty minutes earlier, picked her up in front of her wide-eyed assistant, and carried her to his pickup. Though outwardly she'd protested the Hollywood action, secretly she was swept off her feet in more ways than one.

The fall foliage flew past on either side of the small highway leading out of town, but Esther barely noticed its loveliness. "Okay, I mean it. I want to know where we're going."

"You're not very patient, are you? I hadn't noticed that so much before today."

"That's because you've never *kidnapped* me before today."

He grinned again. "We'll be there in about ten minutes, so just relax."

Scowling, she sat back and crossed her arms, feeling a full pout coming on. "All right, but this is under protest. And it had better be worth it."

"I think you'll be pleasantly surprised," Tom said wryly. He hummed along with the Christian radio station while Esther sat silently taking in the last days of autumn. He maneuvered the truck onto a small gravel road.

89

Esther forgot her protest as she took in the sight of the sun seeping through the red and gold leaves shielding the road like a canopy. She drew in a sharp breath. "Oh, how gorgeous."

He pulled to the end of the road where a field stretched out before them bordered by evergreens and oaks. Tom shifted into park and killed the motor. He got out, walked around to her side of the truck, and opened the door.

"How would you like to have a picnic with me?"

"I'd love it." Placing her hand into his, Esther slid from the seat. Tom moved to the back of the truck and grabbed a picnic basket and a blanket.

A cool breeze lifted Esther's hair and blew across the back of her neck. She shivered.

"Cold?"

It was on the tip of her tongue to say no, but as he put his arm around her and pulled her close, she changed it to, "Not very."

"Now, was it worth it?"

"Every frustrating second. You should know I'm not patient in general. And I'm typically not crazy about surprises."

A laugh rumbled his chest. "You like surprises. You just don't like waiting for the surprise."

Nudging him with her elbow, she gave a sheepish grin. "I guess you're right."

"What a beautiful view. Where did you hear about this place?"

"Here and there." He set the picnic basket on the spread blanket and motioned for her to sit down. She complied, unloading chunk cheese, apple slices, deli sandwiches, and a bottle of sparkling cider. "Wow, you went all out. I'm impressed."

He leaned forward and brushed her lips with a quick kiss. "Good. I like impressing you."

"I like being impressed." Her giddiness emboldened her, and she initiated a return kiss.

Smiling, he sat back. They ate in the serenity of the deserted field, the silence broken occasionally by the call of geese overhead as they gave up their summer homes and traveled south for the winter. Tom glowed with pride as he talked about his grandson. And to Esther's profound relief, he admitted to clearing the air with Minnie after he got home the night before.

Tom pulled her against him, and his arms surrounded her from behind. They watched the breeze move the branches of the outlying trees, sending red and gold leaves floating to the already laden ground. Cradled in Tom's arms, Esther sighed with contentment. The sun caressed her face, and she closed her eyes, relishing the moment.

"I could get used to days like this," Tom whispered against her ear.

"Mmm. Me, too," she replied lazily, stroking the soft hairs on his arm.

"Then let's do it."

"What? Spend our days out here?" She gave a short laugh. "I'd never get any work done."

He pulled back and turned her to face him. "I mean, let's spend the rest of our lives out here."

"What are you talking about?" Understanding was beginning to glimmer, but Esther didn't want to allow herself false hope.

Moving in front of her, Tom knelt and reached into his front jacket pocket. He pulled out a ring box. He took a deep breath. "I know we've only been dating a couple of months, but we've both felt the intensity of the relationship."

Unable to find her voice, Esther simply nodded. There was no doubt what her answer would be. This guy was the embodiment of every dream she'd had.

Apparently taking her silence for hesitation, Tom hurried on, stating his case. "I don't think there's any reason to wait until we've known each other longer. I know enough to love you, and I want to spend my life finding out the rest of the details. This is my land, and if you agree, I'd like to build our house here."

He gathered a breath and commanded her gaze, a hint of anxiety evident in his blue eyes.

Swallowing back tears, Esther threw her whole heart into a loving smile. "I hope you know what you're getting yourself into. I'm pretty set in my ways. I'll probably nag you all the time."

He threw back his head and laughed. "I'll take my chances."

Breathlessly, Esther watched as he opened the ring box. Her eyes widened as she glimpsed the solitaire diamond ring. "It's beautiful."

"It's simple." He pulled it from the box and took hold of her left hand.

The stone sparkled in the sunlight. Anything but simple. This was the most beautiful ring in the world. The cool silver circle slipped over her ring finger, and to Esther it was as though the world had settled into slow motion.

"It's perfect," she said, not taking her eyes off the token of Tom's intent to marry her, to make her dreams of home and family finally come true. "Oh, Tom. You really love me?" She shifted her gaze to his and captured such a look of love shining from him, there was no room for an ounce of doubt. A thrill rose inside of her, and she threw her arms about his neck. He held her in a tight embrace and rose to his feet, lifting her with him.

He held her out at arm's length. "I'd like to announce it at dinner tonight. Is that okay?"

A sudden fear shot through her. "What if they don't want us to get married?"

A laugh escaped him. "Are you kidding me? They're crazy about you. You've even managed to bring Minnie around. Why would they object?"

She shrugged, secretly delighted with his take on her relationship with his children. "Liking me as a friend of their dad's is one thing. Accepting me as the stepmother is entirely different."

Pulling her closer, Tom shook his head. "Trust me, sweetheart. We held a family meeting last night about this. There's not a dissenter in the ranks. You're in."

"You held a family meeting about this?"

"Yes."

"And what if there *had* been a dissenter?"

Lines etched his brow. "Well, I'd have listened to the objections and asked you to marry me anyway. But at least we'd have known who to look out for."

That answer was good enough for her. "All right. Then I guess it's all settled. We'll announce it tonight."

He gathered her closer and dipped his head. His breath mingled with hers a split second before he kissed her. Esther sensed the difference in the intensity of this kiss from all the others. As his lips moved over hers, they claimed her with a promise of what lay ahead for them.

Contentment welled up inside of her. Even in her sweetest dreams of falling in love, she'd never imagined such a feeling. In Tom's embrace, she closed her eyes and enjoyed the moment. She imagined shopping for wedding gowns, furniture, baby doctors, and experiencing all the baby "firsts" she'd never really believed would happen.

❧

"So, how'd it go?"

Freshly showered and moving about his room in stocking feet, Tom held the cordless phone and smiled at the sound of Ashley's voice. "You'll have to wait until dinner to find out. Did you pick up my grandson from the hospital?"

An exasperated sigh filtered over the line. "You're going to make me wait? And yes, I picked up our darling. He's sleeping in his daddy's arms."

Tom could hear the joy in her voice, and his heart lifted at the sound. Thank God for His mercy.

"You know, Dad, if Esther answered your proposal the way I suspect, I wouldn't be a bit surprised if next year, we're expecting a new little baby brother or sister."

A burst of laughter shot from Tom. "Oh, sure. Cute, little girl."

For a moment, silence was his only answer. "Dad, have you and Esther discussed children?"

"We've discussed you kids."

"I mean starting a family of your own."

"I already have a family."

"Esther doesn't."

Tom breathed in a long, cool breath, frowned, then dismissed Ashley's concern. Surely, if Esther wanted children of her own, she would have mentioned it by now. The woman hadn't planned to marry at all until he'd come along, let alone have children.

"Dad? Are you still there?"

"Yeah. Listen, the only children Esther and I have discussed are you kids. Don't you think I'd know if she wanted a baby?"

"I don't know. Probably. Sorry for bringing it up."

"All right, I'll be heading over there in a few minutes. Anything I can bring?"

"Just Esther."

"That goes without saying."

"Okay. Love you, Dad. I can't wait until the announcement."

"Me, either."

Tom couldn't shake Ashley's comments as he finished getting ready. He glanced at the baby photographs on his dresser. First Ashley, then Minnie, and finally Chris. For Tom, their childhoods had been filled with the wonder of learning to parent, teaching them the alphabet, that first bike ride without the training wheels. But he had done all of those things alone.

What *if* Esther wanted to have a baby? Did he have the desire or energy to go through that again? The thought of marriage to Esther filled him with images of passion-filled nights, long walks and talks, companionable retirement years. Never once had he considered the possibility of starting another family. Slipping on his shoes, he tried to reason with himself. Tried to consider the ramifications of fathering a child at this time in his life. What if something were to happen to her like it had his children's mother? Life was so uncertain.

If he and Esther got married soon and had a child right away, he'd be in his late fifties before the kid hit puberty, sixties before graduation. And what if he had another daughter? He'd be hobbling down the aisle with her at her wedding.

His brain echoed a resounding *NO*. He was ready to enjoy his grandson and ready to grow old gracefully with the woman he loved. More children were out of the question. If by any remote possibility Esther had something else in mind, he'd just have to be the voice of reason.

Shaking his head at the absurdity, he grabbed his keys and headed for the door.

A baby?

Not a chance.

ten

"Oh, Kare, look. Isn't this the sweetest thing?"

Esther pulled Karen aside to look at another baby outfit in the downtown shop. Her sister groaned, but followed along as she had numerous times. For the past hour, they'd perused every rack and shelf possible and were now on the second time around. Esther was thrilled with her first visit to the "Oh Baby" store.

"I can't believe I've never shopped here before. This shop is fabulous." She gasped in delight at a tiny red jacket. "Take a look at this. Isn't it precious?"

Karen scowled. "Esther, you're going to go broke if you don't stop grabbing everything you see."

"But it's an itty bitty St. Louis Cardinals jacket. It's so sweet."

Karen looked at the price tag and released an exasperated breath. "Yes and it's sixty-five bucks."

The arrow of reason hit its mark, and Esther replaced the little jacket on the rack. "You're right. But you should just see little Tommy. He's so adorable."

"I'm sure he is," Karen groused. "But you weren't nearly this gah-gah over my kids—and you know there have never been any three children born as cute as mine."

"Of course not," Esther humored, forcing herself to look away from a pair of baby sneakers with a popular logo stitched on the sides. "But when your kids were babies, I was just trying to get my business off the ground and couldn't afford these kinds of presents."

"We always loved whatever you bought—regardless of where you picked it up or how much it cost. Besides, we're supposed to be shopping for wedding gowns, not baby stuff. First things first, remember? First comes love, then comes marriage, *then* comes Esther pushing a baby carriage."

"These aren't for me," Esther insisted. "They're for Ashley's baby. Can't I be a doting stepgrandmother-to-be?"

Laughter bubbled from Karen's lips. "I can't get used to that. You're actually going to be a grandmother." She sobered and lowered her tone. "Have you and Tom discussed children of your own?"

A frown puckered Esther's brow. "No. Tom is very happy with his life. His daughters are grown and Chris graduates this year. He's settled, you know? I'm pretty sure he doesn't want to have any more children."

"Well, how do you know for sure if you haven't discussed it with him?"

She shrugged, wishing Karen would just drop it. Not that she hadn't thought about the same thing every waking moment since he'd proposed, but voicing her concerns made them real, and she didn't want anything to spoil her lovely maternal fantasies. "A woman just knows."

"Oh, please."

Esther glanced at the determination on her sister's face and decided she might as well open up.

"Okay, for instance, the other night we had dinner with his kids to welcome the new baby home. He made a point of saying how much he loved little Tommy and how he gets to do all the fun baby stuff and then send him home with his mom and dad."

"Ouch. Well, did you tell him you want to have a baby of your own?"

Tears stung Esther's eyes, but she blinked them away as

they approached the counter. After making her purchases for Tommy, she stayed quiet until they left the baby store and hit the pavement, headed toward the bridal shop a few doors down.

"Now, there are no sales ladies listening," Karen said. "Have you spoken with Tom about this?"

Esther shook her head, and this time the tears came faster than she could blink them away.

Karen slipped her arm around Esther's shoulders. "Really, Esther, you can't go another day without talking to him."

"It's more than that. I—I'm not sure I can even have any."

"Okay, stop. Let's get a cup of coffee and talk about this before we go look at wedding gowns." Karen took hold of her arm and led her into a café.

"All right," Karen said, as soon as they had their lattes and as much privacy as the crowded café allowed. "What makes you think you might not be able to have children?"

"It's been two months since. . ." Esther hesitated and glanced around the room. She leaned forward and lowered her voice. "You know. . ."

Karen's expression registered understanding, and she nodded. Then her brow puckered. "You couldn't be pregnant, could you?"

"How can you even ask that? Tom and I are committed to God and to staying pure until the wedding."

"Esther, there could be a million reasons. Don't automatically assume. . ."

"This isn't the first time I've missed. It's been happening a lot this year."

"Then you need to go see your doctor and find out what's going on."

"I know. I'm just afraid of what she's going to tell me."

Karen chewed her bottom lip, a telltale sign she wanted to

say something she wasn't sure Esther was going to want to hear. Esther braced herself. "What, Kare?"

"Okay. I was just wondering if you've given any more thought to foster parenting. Before you met Tom, you were convinced God was leading you to go through the training and get your license. Seems a shame to let all that go to waste."

Esther sat back in the booth, her fingers tracing the rim of her coffee mug. "I'd still love to do it. But I have Tom to consider now. I'm not sure he even wants more children of his own. How could I ask him to be a foster parent?"

"I understand. It's just that we need foster parents badly, and I noticed that all your paperwork is up to date in the office. You're ready to go."

"I am?" A sense of excitement rose inside Esther. The old enthusiasm.

"Yes. If you've decided against foster parenting, you should call the office so we can take you off the list of potential homes."

Esther hesitated. "I don't feel right about that. But to be honest, I'm not sure if it's guilt or a desperate need to share my life with a child and the knowledge that this might be my only chance to do that." Tears stung her eyes once more. "What if I can't carry a baby of my own, Kare? It seems so unfair."

Karen reached across the table and took her hand. She bowed her head and prayed for Esther to have peace, for God to be in control of everything concerning the situation, for Esther to have the courage to open up to the man with whom she'd agreed to share her life.

They were both crying by the time Karen said, "Amen."

⁂

Tom sat in the parking lot of the women's clinic, waiting for Ashley to come out. Since no one else was available to watch Tommy during her checkup, Tom had agreed to come along.

But the parking lot was where he drew the line. If not for

the baby getting his picture taken right after Ashley's appointment, Tom wouldn't have come within two miles of the women's clinic. Especially considering the worrisome thoughts rolling around in his mind lately. So far, all of his hints about being too old to have a new baby of his own had failed to bring about the reaction from Esther he'd hoped for—agreement.

In fact, she'd been noncommittal each time he'd broached the topic, which led him to believe that Ashley may have been right when she suggested Esther would want to have a baby of her own.

Scrubbing his hands over his face, he let out a groan. He didn't want to do anything to jeopardize his relationship with Esther, but having another child was out of the question.

He glanced through the windshield, willing Ashley to hurry up. He felt ill at ease sitting in this parking lot. No matter where he looked, he saw women walking to and from their cars. Not even one male doctor walked through the parking lot. It made him feel like a peeping. . .well. . .Tom.

And every time he saw a dark-haired woman, he did a double-take, thinking it was Esther. Like the one walking out of the clinic right now. He frowned and peered closer as the woman headed toward the pharmacy—she was a dead ringer. *Wait a minute.* That *was* Esther.

He honked. She turned, scanned the lot, then froze when she saw him. Mindful of the baby, Tom knew he couldn't go to her, so he rolled down the window and waved her over.

"Hi," she said, a little breathless from her fast walk across the lot.

Tom's throat tightened as he searched Esther's face. Her eyes were red as though she'd been crying, and the absence of makeup cinched his suspicion.

"What's wrong?"

"What do you mean?"

"Besides the fact that you're filling a prescription, which we'll get to in a minute, I can tell you've been crying. Is everything all right?"

She waved his question aside. "Just emotional, woman stuff."

"Woman stuff, huh?" As much as he'd like to pursue the matter, to make her realize there was nothing she couldn't share with him, he knew a brush-off line when he heard it. But he understood her timidity about such a personal topic. Tenderness swelled his chest. She had never had a real relationship with a man before, and he couldn't expect her to open up about private female matters so soon.

Eyes glowing, Esther spared him the necessity of the next line of conversation. "Oh, look who you have with you." Her expression softened as she peered in at Tommy. "He's growing so fast."

"Blink your eyes and he grows an inch," he answered with a wry grin. "His mother is here for her checkup, and she needed a baby-sitter."

"That explains it. I thought maybe you were following me."

"I'm not. But I am a little curious. Are you okay? Physically, I mean."

Tom could tell it took quite the effort for her to drag her gaze from the baby and focus on him. "I'm fine. Why do you ask?" Was it his imagination, or did she seem a little defensive?

"You were going into the pharmacy. I thought maybe you were getting medicine."

A blush stained her cheeks. "Oh. Just filling a prescription."

"For?"

"Something personal." She smiled in an effort, he surmised, to take the sting from the "none-of-your-business" response.

"As long as you're fine."

"I am. But I need to pick up my prescription and get back to work." She leaned forward and kissed him lightly.

"Do you want to have dinner with me tonight?"

Her brow rose. "I thought you were going bowling with the men from church."

"I could change my plans."

"Oh, don't do that," she said quickly, a little too quickly as far as he was concerned. But she said it with such a beautiful smile, that he couldn't hold a grudge. "To tell you the truth, I sort of looked forward to ordering Chinese food and curling up with my new novel."

"Sounds a little lonely to me."

She let out a short laugh. "Not to me. I haven't read a book in ages."

Stung to be replaced by words on a page, he nevertheless forced a smile and nodded. "All right. I can take a hint," he said, only half teasing.

She started to step back, but he slipped his hand behind her head and drew her to him for another kiss. She responded to his embrace, but pulled away sooner than he would have liked.

"I'll see you later," she whispered.

A sense of foreboding hit him full in the gut as he watched her go. He didn't like the fact that she was keeping something from him. The thought struck him that he didn't really know her very well. Only three months. Had they moved too fast? His love-struck heart warred with the reason that had failed him since he'd met Esther. Was he doing the right thing? Or was he making the biggest mistake of his life?

❧

"So what did the doctor say?" Karen's call interrupted Esther's pity party. She sat wearing her *I love Goofy* T-shirt and her comfy sweats. She'd already downed way too much sweet-and-sour chicken, wontons, and at least three egg rolls. So now, the pain in her stomach rivaled the pain in her heart.

One week after her first appointment, Esther had returned for test results. The doctor had given her wretched news as far as she was concerned. "Perimenopause," she said dully.

"What?"

Esther sniffed and swiped at the fresh onslaught of tears with the back of her hand. "Perimenopause. That's what my doctor thinks is going on."

"Aren't you a little young for that?" Karen said, indignation edging her tone. "Maybe you should get another opinion."

"No, a lot of women in their late thirties and early forties get it. It's sort of a prelude to the actual full-blown thing."

"Wait. Honey. Calm down a second. I don't completely understand."

Esther gulped back a sob. "It means I'm getting old. The train's passed me by. Over the hill. Always a grandmother, never a mother. Does that make it any clearer?"

"The doctor said you can't have a baby? That doesn't make sense. Women older than you are having babies all the time."

"Yeah, well, some people have all the luck."

"You have no options?" Karen pressed.

"Fertility drugs to increase my chances each month; luck of the draw. Typical stuff for infertile couples."

"Well, see? It's not impossible."

Esther sighed and touched her palm to her forehead. "The doctor said I shouldn't put it off too long if I plan to get pregnant."

"Then you'll just have to talk it over with Tom right away."

A groan escaped as she voiced the thoughts she'd been avoiding for the past few hours—ever since she'd run into Tom in the clinic parking lot. "How can I ask him to go through all that trouble?"

"Esther, Tom knows you two aren't college-aged kids. If

you're going to start a family, you don't have time to wait. That has to have been on his mind, too."

"I don't know."

"Well, sweetie, I don't have to tell you this, but it bears saying." Karen hesitated, then went on. "You need to talk to Tom. The sooner the better."

eleven

The first thing Tom noticed when Esther walked through the door, her arms laden with gifts for Tommy, was her tight smile. The sense of foreboding that had nudged him a few days earlier now kicked into high gear and slammed into his gut like a line drive traveling a hundred miles per hour.

He relieved her of the oversized load. "All this for one little baby?"

"Be glad my sister was with me, or I might have bought out the whole store." Shrugging out of her black leather, full-length coat, Esther gave him a sheepish grin, one that put him a little more at ease. He leaned down and kissed her upturned lips.

"Are Ashley and Trevor here yet?"

"Yep, they're in the family room with Minnie and Mitch. Chris should be home anytime."

"Thank you for inviting me for dinner before the shower guests arrive." Her smile lit up the shadowy places of his heart, and he felt a sudden sense of rightness. He'd most likely been overreacting to her vagueness.

"Look who's here, everyone." His announcement was unnecessary as Minnie and Ashley had already left their seats to give Esther welcoming hugs.

Watching his daughters interact with his future wife boosted Tom's optimism even higher. He inwardly mocked himself for being such a worrywart.

Esther glanced about the room. "Where's the baby?"

"Napping," Ashley replied. "Although I doubt he will be

for much longer if the guys don't stop yelling at the TV."

"So who's playing?" Esther asked.

"Bears and Rams."

"Yeah, the Bears are getting creamed. But then, that's nothing new." Minnie tossed a sideways glance at Mitch and grinned.

"Just wait. The Bears are a great come-from-behind team. They'll pull it off." It was common knowledge that Mitch rooted for all the Chicago teams—out of loyalty, Tom suspected, to his grandparents who had lived in Chicago their entire lives.

As usual, Minnie couldn't resist pushing his buttons. Why that kid put up with her, Tom couldn't fathom, but they'd been best friends since childhood and Mitch never held a grudge. After a couple more derogatory comments aimed at the Bears, Minnie squealed as Mitch had all he could take without retaliation. Tom grinned in satisfaction as the kid pulled Minnie into a headlock and began knuckling her head. "Say the Bears rule."

"Never!"

"Say it!" Mitch doubled his efforts.

"Okay, okay. The Bears. . ." Mitch relaxed his hold. Minnie twisted out of his grip and tossed a victorious grin from half a room away. ". . .stink!" Turning, she sprinted from the room.

Chaos ensued as Mitch took out after her.

Tom shook his head and laughed, meeting Esther's amused gaze. "What are they, fourteen years old?" he asked.

"Don't wake up the baby!" Ashley called.

As though nothing out of the ordinary had occurred, Trevor kept his attention glued to the game.

"Want to go into the kitchen for some coffee? It would give us a few minutes alone to catch up on the last couple of days," Tom asked, slipping his arm around her slender waist.

Esther nodded. "Sounds lovely."

In the kitchen, she sat at the table while he poured two cups full of freshly made coffee. When he set them down, Esther glanced at him with a knowing smile. "I think you're going to be walking another daughter down the aisle before too long."

Tom blinked at her, trying to absorb her meaning.

Apparently picking up on his bewilderment, Esther laughed.

"Isn't it obvious? Mitch is crazy about Minnie." She shook a pink packet of artificial sweetener into her cup and stirred. "I can't believe you haven't noticed before now."

He shook his head. "You're way off base. They're just friends. Ask either of them."

"Trust me." She lifted her chin stubbornly. "Mitch is head-over-heals in love."

Amused affection surged inside of Tom's breast. He leaned over and kissed her cheek. "You're cute. But, believe me, I know those two. Minnie is madly in love with Greg, and Mitch is in love with video games and math."

"Okay, have it your way. But when they announce their engagement, I expect a formal apology."

"It'll never happen, but if it does, I'll send an apology over the radio and dedicate a song to you."

"I'll hold you to it."

A burst of cold air shot through the kitchen as Minnie pushed open the door and stomped inside, soaking wet and shivering. "Can you believe that jerk?"

"What happened?" Tom asked. He was about to close the door when Mitch came in after her.

"He hosed me," she said, glaring at the offender. "In the middle of winter. He doesn't care if I die of pneumonia!"

Rolling his eyes at her dramatics, Tom cast a disparaging

glance at the puddle of water at her feet. "You're dripping all over the place. Better go upstairs and change."

She sent Mitch another glare and stalked away, but not without the last word. "Jerk!"

"Bears rule!" Mitch called after her, obviously unaffected by her anger.

"They stink!" she called back from the steps.

Mitch shrugged at Tom, swiped a muffin from the counter, and headed back to the family room.

Sending Esther a triumphant grin, Tom sat back and folded his arms over his chest. "Oh, yeah. They're just a step away from matrimony."

"I'm more convinced than ever that those two are meant for each other." A knowing smile curved her lips. "You might want to write out that apology so you don't get all tongue-tied once you're on the air."

Tom joined her laugher. Watching her sip her coffee across from him, he envisioned years of doing this very thing morning after morning. They would grow old together, enjoying each other's company. He sighed with contentment.

❧

Esther looked down at the baby in her arms and swallowed hard, trying to keep the tears at bay. She'd volunteered to hold him to give Ashley a chance to eat a warm meal. While Esther rocked the baby in the wooden rocker, she couldn't help but pretend Tommy was hers. Hers and Tom's.

The scents of brown-and-serve dinner rolls mingling with the spicy smells of homemade lasagna made her stomach grumble. But Esther wouldn't have traded this moment for anything—even if she were starving to death.

When Ashley peeked into the room a little while later, Esther wasn't even close to ready to let the baby go, but he

was beginning to stir and root around. "You're just in time."
She smiled at Ashley. "I think he's hungry."

Ashley nodded. "I thought he'd be about ready to eat.
Thanks so much. It was nice to make it through a full meal
uninterrupted."

"My pleasure." Esther stood and handed the baby over.

"Dad said you should go eat now before Mitch and Trevor
devour all the lasagna."

Esther chuckled. "I'm going." She leaned over and kissed
the baby's head.

Ashley sat in the rocker. "Esther, can I ask a nosy question?"

"Of course."

The girl opened her mouth, then hesitation flickered in
her eyes and she shook her head. "Never mind. It's none of
my business."

"Are you sure? I don't usually mind nosy questions."

A smiled curved Ashley's lips. "No. I better stay out of it."

Curiosity simmered, but Esther decided to let it go. If the
girl was that hesitant, maybe she was right and this wasn't a
topic Esther wanted to discuss with her future stepdaughter.

"All right. I better go eat so I can help clean up before your
guests start to arrive."

"I'm looking forward to seeing Karen again."

"Thanks. I know she's looking forward to seeing you, too."
Karen had recently begun attending the contemporary service, and she and Ashley had hit it off right away. "I'll see
you in a little while."

Esther made her way back to the kitchen, a little nostalgic
over her empty arms. She could still feel the warmth of
Tommy's little body. A heavy sigh escaped, but she pulled it
together before joining the merriment coming from the
group sitting around the table. She forced a smile and
stepped into the room.

"Finally, Esther." Chris stood and held onto the chair next to him. She smiled at him and took the seat. "I need someone on my side, Esther."

"I'll help if I can."

"I think it's only fair that you and dad give me a baby brother or sister."

Esther felt a jolt go through her, and she had to fight not to spew the sip of iced tea she'd just taken. "W—what?"

"I've been the youngest kid around here all my life. But now that Dad's marrying a younger woman, I think we need an addition. What do you say?"

Esther felt everyone's eyes upon her. Heat rose to her cheeks, and she tried to cover her horror by coming up with an evasive, yet witty remark. "Actually, I'm not much younger than your dad," she murmured, keeping her gaze firmly fixed on her plate of lasagna. Not exactly witty, but evasive nonetheless.

"Leave her alone, Chris." Esther glanced up at the sound of Tom's voice. His tone was harsher than she'd ever heard.

"Sorry, Esther," the teen mumbled. "I was just kidding."

"Sometimes your teasing goes too far." Tom's tone remained stern.

Esther caught his gaze and looked away from the questioning and dread she saw in the blue depths. Her appetite fled and she stood. "I'll clean up. The rest of you better go hang balloons. Everyone will start arriving in an hour."

"What about your supper?" Tom looked up at her.

"I'm not very hungry." She couldn't bear to look him in the eye. Couldn't bear the thought that he might be reading her thoughts and have completely different ideas about their future together.

Surely, God wouldn't allow her to fall in love with a man who couldn't or wouldn't give her a baby.

Tom herded the kids out of the kitchen and gave express orders for them to get the balloons done—without filling them with water first. He joined Esther in cleaning up. They worked together removing dishes from the table, putting leftovers away, and wiping down counters. He swept the kitchen floor while she loaded the dishwasher.

Their conversation remained light, a deliberate ploy, he suspected, to avoid a return to the topic Chris had broached—a topic he knew was going to have to be discussed very soon. She'd appeared noncommittal, and he couldn't gauge whether or not she agreed with Chris about giving the boy a baby brother or sister. He might have been joking, but that sudden light in Esther's eyes had been anything but funny. Surely, God wouldn't have allowed him to fall in love with a woman who wanted a child that he simply had no desire to father at this time in his life.

twelve

"These kids really need you, Esther." Karen's voice broke and even through the phone line, Esther could tell she was crying. "I don't want to send them just anywhere. Please? For me?"

"I just don't know, Kare. My life is so complicated right now." Resting her elbow on the desk, she pressed the heel of her hand to her forehead. She hated how selfish she sounded. But how could she take care of two kids when her own life was so uncertain?

"Just for tonight? You have that spare bedroom sitting there empty. I promise, I'll try to place them somewhere else tomorrow."

Releasing a heavy sigh, Esther felt her resolve waning. "All right. Give me a couple of hours to go shopping before you bring them over."

"Okay. I can keep them occupied that long. Thanks."

She pushed the button to get a dial tone and called Tom. Ashley answered. "Pearson Lumber."

"Hi, Ashley. It's Esther. Is your dad there?"

"Hi, Esther. He's out on a call right now. Want me to give him a message?"

"Yeah. Tell him I'm going to have to cancel our plans for tonight. Something came up."

"He'll be disappointed. But I'll tell him."

Esther gathered her belongings and left instructions for her assistant to lock up at closing time. Then she went to the grocery store to buy some kid-friendly cereal and snacks.

The children, a boy, aged five, and a girl, barely out of

diapers, had just become wards of the state after their mother was arrested and put in jail. According to Karen, the little boy had been taking care of them both for three days when a neighbor discovered them alone. Their mother had been found strung out in a crack house. No one knew who the father—or fathers—were and as far as anyone knew, the children had no other family.

Esther raged inside at the unfairness of it all. Why did God allow unfit people to have kids when decent people who would love and take care of them couldn't have children? She rejected the idea that maybe she should stop worrying about whether she could have her own baby or not and just adopt one of the many wards of the state who had no one to call Mommy.

It wasn't that she didn't sympathize with those precious children; it was just that she wanted her own flesh and blood. She wanted to feel a baby growing inside of her, wanted to know the joy of nursing her child at her breast. Adoption would feel like. . .settling, somehow.

She picked up the groceries, bubble bath, junior-sized toothbrushes, then, on a whim, headed to the toy department and loaded a cart with cars, dolls, books, and art supplies. She knew it was only for one night. But the thought of what those children must have gone through compelled her to provide things she was sure they'd done without in their short lives. Toys were more than a luxury. For children, they were a necessity.

Arriving home a solid hour before they were due, Esther cut premixed cookie dough and placed it onto a baking sheet. Once the treats were in the oven, she hurried to unload the rest of the groceries. She put the toys in the bedroom where the children would sleep and ran to shower and change out of her work clothes. She'd just finished drying her hair when the doorbell rang. Her heart lurched as she headed to the door.

The sight of the children nearly took her breath away. Karen stood behind a dark-haired little boy. His wide brown eyes stared up at her with uncertainty and even a bit of fear. Her maternal instincts ran into overload, and she offered him a smile. Much to Esther's delight, he returned the smile without reservation, showing surprisingly lovely baby teeth. The little girl clung to Karen as Esther stepped aside to allow the little troupe entry.

With gentle hands, Karen pulled the little girl free and handed her to Esther. Rather than scream and fight, the child transferred her stranglehold from one woman to the other.

"Children, this is Miss Esther and, as I told you earlier, she's going to be taking care of you tonight." Karen turned to Esther. "That's Tonya. She's two and a half and still has accidents, so I brought some diapers for overnight. And this," she said, ruffling the boy's hair, "is Chuck. He's five and very, very smart. Which you'll find out for yourself soon enough."

"Very nice to meet you both," Esther said, her heart wrapping around the warm little body in her arms and extending to Chuck, who seemed to be relaxing with each passing second.

"I made some cookies. Do you like chocolate chip?"

Chuck nodded vigorously.

"Did you plan supper for them?" Karen asked. "They haven't eaten yet."

"Hmm. I didn't think to start supper."

Disappointment and resignation passed over Chuck's features. Esther's stomach sank. The child obviously believed he'd be going without since she'd forgotten about dinner. How many meals had these children missed?

"I'll order pizza."

She grinned as his eyes widened.

Karen chuckled. "You're going to be popular. Cookies and pizza."

Esther waggled her eyebrows. "I have toys and coloring books, too."

"That's a lot of stuff for overnight guests."

"They can take them with them tomorrow." She knew Karen had thought she'd take one look at these angelic children, then agree to keep them as long as need be, but Esther wasn't ready to commit to that.

Karen gave her a disappointed scowl. "All right," she said. "There are two outfits each in the bag along with underwear and socks and PJs. I got them out of the freebie bags we have at the office."

Esther nodded. "Do you have time for some coffee?"

"No. I need to get home and feed my family. Besides, this will give you and the children time to get to know each other. I'll call you in the morning."

After giving Esther a quick hug, Karen patted Tonya's back and, once again, ruffled Chuck's hair before leaving.

"All right then, how about I call and order a pizza and we can get to know each other? How's that sound?"

"Good."

She tried to set Tonya down, but the child clung to her like a spider monkey. She pressed a kiss to the child's dark head and laughed. "Come on, Chuck. Do you know your numbers?"

He nodded. "Uh-huh."

Esther smiled. "Then you get to push the buttons on the telephone."

A sparkle of excitement lit his beautiful eyes and Esther's heart soared.

After ordering pizza, she turned to Chuck. "Can you grab the bag Miss Karen brought your things in? I'll show you to your room."

"See how strong I am?" Chuck asked, muscling the bag with one hand.

"Wow, you're a big guy. I'm lucky to have you around here."

The boy beamed under her praise.

"Follow me, strong man."

Esther's arms felt like lead, and Tonya's stranglehold was beginning to feel stifling. She hoped like crazy the toys would entice the child to let go.

"Is this my room?" Chuck asked, wonder thick in his voice.

"Yes. You and your sister's. Do you like it?"

He nodded, setting the bag on the bed. "Can I get on it?"

"The bed?"

"Uh-huh."

"Of course you can."

He climbed up, then didn't seem to quite know what to do. He glanced around and squirmed.

"Tonya, honey, would you like to sit next to your brother on the bed? I have some presents for you."

She tried to pry the child away, but she clung tighter.

"Don't you want to see your new toys?"

Feeling the little arms relax, Esther sighed in relief and took the opportunity to set the toddler next to her brother. She went to the closet and pulled out the bags filled with toys. She took them to the bed.

"Who gets them?" Chuck asked.

"You do, of course. Do you see any other boys in this room who might like this remote-controlled jeep?"

Wide-eyed, Chuck shook his head.

She pulled a soft, blond-haired, blue-eyed doll from a bag and stretched it toward Tonya. The little girl looked at her in wonderment and took the toy with painstaking slowness as though she expected Esther to change her mind and rescind the offer.

Esther's throat clogged as Tonya clutched the doll to her chest, her beautiful face split into a wide smile.

"What do you say, Tonya?" Chuck demanded, scowling at his sister.

"Thank you," Tonya whispered.

Esther ran her hand over the little girl's silken curls. "You're welcome, sweetheart."

Chuck nodded like a placated parent. Esther didn't have the heart to inform the boy that he had failed to thank her for his toys. Thanks weren't important today. Making the kids feel welcome, wanted, and safe mattered most. Manners could be dealt with later.

She sat back on the bed and watched while the children played. As soon as the children were asleep, she was going to call Karen. There was no way these children were going anywhere. In fact, her mind was already beginning to whirl with plans. In the morning, she was going to call the office and have some work faxed over so she could work from home while she worked out child-care details.

Her heart leapt with the possibilities. The only question was. . .what would Tom say?

❧

Tom made a slight detour on his way home. When Ashley told him Esther had to cancel their date for that night, he'd been more than disappointed. He'd become worried. A quick call to her office had yielded very little information from Missy, Esther's assistant. All she could tell him was that Esther had gotten a call from her sister and shortly thereafter had gone home for the day.

Tom wasn't sure what to make of the news. He'd tried to call earlier, but there had been no answer. The next time, the line had been busy, so he knew she was home. Rather than call again and take a chance that she'd brush him off, he decided to drive by her house. Just long enough to assure himself that she was all right. She'd been acting strangely lately. . .and there was that pharmacy incident. What if something were seriously wrong? Would she tell him?

He pulled his truck behind her car and headed to the porch. It took a couple of minutes for her to answer when he rang the bell.

"Tom. I thought you were the pizza guy."

"You cancelled our date so you could stay home and order a pizza?" Hurt and bewilderment pushed at his heart.

Releasing a heavy sigh, she moved aside and opened the door wider. "Of course not. Come in. What brings you by that couldn't have been answered over the phone?"

Defenses rising, Tom stepped inside and glanced around. Nothing seemed out of the ordinary, unless he considered the scent of freshly baked cookies hanging in the air. "You've been acting differently lately. I just need to see for myself that you're all right."

"Well, as you can see. . ."

Tom peered close. She seemed a little nervous, but not necessarily in a bad way. She had a glow about her that he wasn't sure he'd noticed before.

"Okay. I'm not leaving until you talk to me. Tell me what's happening between us." He took her hand. "Are you having second thoughts about marrying me?"

Her eyes widened and her mouth dropped open. "Oh, no, Tom." She moved easily and naturally into his arms. Tom closed his eyes and buried his face in the tender curve of her neck. He breathed in deeply, taking comfort in her familiar scent as relief spread through him.

He wasn't sure what made him open his eyes, but a sense that something in the room had changed prompted him to do just that. The sight that met him caused an immediate jumble of confusing thoughts. He stepped back, but didn't look at Esther. Rather, he looked beyond her to the little boy holding tightly to a toy jeep with one hand and the other draped around the shoulders of a little curly-headed toddler. A beautiful little girl holding tightly to a doll.

"I need to explain something." She gathered a deep breath. "These are foster children. I—I got licensed to foster parent before we met. Karen called me today and needed a place for Chuck and Tonya. Well, just look at them. I couldn't say no."

Foster children? Dragging his gaze from the children, he faced the woman he loved—the woman with whom he wanted to spend the rest of his life, the woman who had been keeping secrets. The sense of foreboding that had been a constant companion of the past couple of weeks now morphed into a stinging sense of betrayal.

The doorbell rang while he was trying to digest the information. Esther roused herself and smiled at the children. "Now that's the pizza for sure."

Tom watched her navigate around him, grab a check off the table next to the door, and take care of the pizza delivery boy.

"Do you want to stay for dinner, Tom? We can talk after I bathe the children and put them to bed."

"I don't think so." He couldn't. He needed time to process. "I'll call you later."

"I'd prefer to discuss this in person," she said tight-lipped.

"How about dinner tomorrow night?"

Her gaze dropped to the pizza box in her arms. "I'll have the children."

"Then, like I said, I'll call you."

Her expression crashed and she nodded. "All right," she whispered. "Call me."

Tom walked to his truck as if in a daze. He needed to think—to sort it all out. Foster children were temporary, right? Kids came, stayed for a little while, then returned to their parents. But something in the memory of Esther's expression when she gazed upon those children answered all the questions he'd been warring with. Even if she gave these two back, she was definitely going to want children.

Sick at heart, Tom drove to the site of their new home. The foundation was laid, walls were up. But he had the sad feeling he wouldn't be carrying Esther over the threshold.

thirteen

"Esther, it's been four weeks since you and Tom broke up. Don't you think it's time to get back on the merry-go-round?"

Rolling her eyes, Esther hugged the phone tighter against her ear with her shoulder and fastened a piece of tape to the umpteenth Christmas present she'd wrapped that night. "The only merry-go-round I ever intend to set foot on again is the kind my lovely children will enjoy."

"*Your* children, huh? Be careful, Esther. Remember their mother will get out of prison in a couple of years. You have to keep that in mind."

Esther's stomach tightened with dread at the very thought of that future day when she'd be forced to hand over Chuck and Tonya. "I don't see how any rational judge can allow a woman like that to have her children back."

"That's what rehabilitation is all about. She'll get clean, take parenting and job-skill training, and most likely be given another chance to do right by those kids."

"If she doesn't end up back in a crack house the second she gets out of jail."

"Well, for Chuck and Tonya's sakes, let's hope that doesn't happen."

"What if they don't want to go back? They'll have been with me a long time by then. Tonya probably won't even remember her."

The line crackled, the only sound between the airways for a few long seconds. Worry clung to Karen's voice when she finally broke the silence. "Maybe I should find them another

122

home. I think you're getting so attached that you can't be reasoned with."

"No, don't be silly," she said quickly. "There's no point making them suffer just because I'm falling in love with them."

"All right. But be rational. If you get to the point where you think it's getting too intense, let me know."

"I promise. Are you all set for tomorrow morning?"

"Of course. Presents are wrapped and under the tree. Turkey is thawing in the fridge, as it has been for the past couple of days. Pies are baked. All we need now are you, Chuck and Tonya, and Dad, of course."

"We'll be there after the kids open all their presents and get some time to play with their new toys. I'm making blueberry pancakes for breakfast. Chuck saw them on a commercial the other day and asked if I knew how to make them." Esther smiled, remembering how the boy obviously hadn't wanted to come right out and ask her for them. She'd decided right then that they would be a surprise Christmas breakfast.

"That sounds good. I might show up over there for breakfast."

"The more the merrier, sister dear." She yawned. "I better go. I still have presents to finish and a camcorder to check out and make sure it's charged up."

"Okay. Make sure you get a shot of their faces when they see all the presents. And bring the tape with you so we can see it."

"I will."

Esther set the phone back on the charger. Tomorrow would be wonderful, and she couldn't wait to see the joy on their little faces when they saw the gifts she'd bought.

The clock struck midnight by the time she finished her wrapping and cleaned up the evidence.

With a yawn, she reached for the light switch just as the phone chirped, nearly sending her through the roof.

A glance at caller ID sent her heart racing. "Hello."

"Merry Christmas."

Esther's stomach flip-flopped at the low tones of Tom's voice.

"Merry Christmas, Tom."

"I'm sorry to call so late, but I knew you were up."

"Oh? How'd you know that?"

"I saw the light on."

Esther ran to the front window, and her heart sank when she didn't see Tom's truck.

"You drove by?"

"Yes."

"You could have stopped."

His wonderful chuckle sent a rush of longing through her. "I would have justified a kiss under the mistletoe, but that would have only made things more difficult for us."

And what do you think this call is doing to me? Esther's heart cried out. She missed him. With every inch of her being. Missed his easy laughter, the conversation at the end of the day. His smile, his arms, his lingering kisses.

"I thought of you yesterday," he said softly.

It was to have been their wedding day.

"I thought of you, too." Her voice broke under threat of tears. "I'm sorry things worked out the way they did."

"Me, too, sweetheart. I blame myself for assuming you were at the same place in life as me just because you're close to my age."

"You're not to blame. I suspected you wouldn't want children for some time before we actually had that last conversation."

Silence hung over the line, long and dreadfully loud. Finally, Tom spoke. "Well, I suppose I should go. Ashley and Trevor are coming over early, and Trevor's folks are joining us later for Christmas dinner. The kids miss you."

"I miss them, too. Please wish them all a merry Christmas from me."

"I will."

ঽ৶

Tom pressed the button to disconnect the call. He'd driven home during his conversation with Esther and now sat in front of his house, truck motor running. With a sigh, he killed the engine and headed inside. The soft glow of the television caught his attention and he headed to the family room. Minnie sat on the couch, a diet soda in front of her, a veggie plate next to it. He had to hand it to the girl, she'd set her mind to losing weight and was doing a super job of sticking with it.

"Hi," he said softly, so as not to startle her.

She turned. "Hey, where'd you go? I thought we'd watch *It's a Wonderful Life* together, but you left."

He shrugged and sank into the overstuffed recliner. "Just driving around."

She nodded. "Holidays are the hardest on those unlucky in love."

"I guess."

"I see Esther at the gym all the time. You should see those kids. They're adorable."

His lips twisted into a wry grin. "I have seen them. And it's not about cute kids. It's about kids in general."

"Chris ruined you for anymore, huh? Can't say that I blame you."

Tom laughed. "You kids are great. Any father would be proud to have a dozen just like you. It's just too late in life to start from scratch."

"Not for men. Look at all those old movie stars marrying young wives and becoming fathers ten and twenty years older than you are."

He'd thought of it. Over and over. Until, for awhile, it was all he could think about. A surefire way to get Esther back would be to give in and agree to have a child. But that was a deceitful way to get what he wanted, and he was afraid he'd resent the baby. Resent every cry, every diaper change, every feeding that took Esther away from him. Perhaps he'd grown selfish over the years, but now wasn't the time to become tied down to that sort of responsibility. This was the time in life when men bought sports cars and took up golfing. Midlife didn't have to be a crisis. He looked forward to it—without little ones, and, unfortunately, without the woman he loved.

ॐ

Esther woke up at four AM and couldn't go back to sleep in anticipation of Chuck and Tonya's responses. She went to the couch and readied the camera for when the time came. By four-thirty, her eyelids began to droop. The next thing she knew, she was being awakened by light streaming through the window. She jerked awake. Expecting to find empty boxes and scattered wrapping paper, she sat up, bewildered to find Chuck and Tonya sitting together in the chair, quietly looking at a book.

"Merry Christmas, kids! Look at all the presents waiting under the tree."

"Yeah," Chuck said glumly.

"Well, honey, don't you want to open them?"

"They're not for us."

Esther frowned. "Come here and sit with me."

The children complied.

"What makes you think those presents aren't for you?"

"Mom said Santa didn't bring presents to kids like us."

A horrified gasp escaped. Esther couldn't help it. "Kids like you? What do you mean?"

He shrugged. "Poor kids."

"Chuck, do you remember how we learned the letters to your name?"

"Yes."

"I want you to go over to that tree and look on the presents. See if you can find your name."

Tentatively, almost as though he were afraid, Chuck moved to the tree. Tonya climbed into Esther's lap and watched her brother with curiosity, but no expectation.

Esther held her breath as he located a gift she knew had his name written on it. He turned to her, a wide grin splitting his dear, sweet face. "C-H-U-C-K. That's me, right? It says Chuck?"

Tears burned her eyes, but she forced them away. "That's right, honey. I want you to tear into that paper."

"Does Tonya have one, too?"

Hugging the little girl to her, she laughed. "Are you kidding? One? There are lots of presents under that tree for you both!" She rose and carried Tonya to the tree. Kneeling, she set the little girl down and started doling out the gifts. Amid the children's squeals of delight, she shook her head in wonder. How could she have ever considered adoption as settling for second best? No other children on earth compared to the two right here in her living room.

≈

"You want to what?" Karen's incredulous tone was to be expected, and Esther took no offense.

"Adopt them," she replied, keeping her tone deliberately even.

Karen pulled a pan of dinner rolls from the oven and set them on a cooling rack. "These children are not up for adoption, Esther. They have a mother."

"A mother who told them Santa didn't bring presents to kids like them. Do you realize this is the first real Christmas they've ever had? It would be cruel to send them back."

In frustration, Karen tossed the oven mitts to the counter and spun to face Esther. "That's not our place to decide. It's not our decision. Don't you remember any of your training?"

"Oh, who cares about that? You can't train the heart who and who not to love." Esther's throat clogged, and she felt tears burn her eyes. "And I love those children. They belong with me."

"Listen. I can ask around. It's possible she would sign over rights if she knew someone wanted them. I'll check into it for you."

"You will?"

Karen gave her a tender smile. "Yeah. Merry Christmas. But don't get your hopes up."

"You might as well tell me not to breathe."

"I know."

The doorbell rang.

Esther frowned. "Are you expecting company?"

"Now, Esther, don't get mad, okay?"

"What are you talking about?"

"I invited Victor for Christmas dinner. His family lives in New York and he didn't have time to go home."

"Victor?"

"The guy from the office?" Karen shook her head. "The social worker who started about the time you met Tom?"

"Oh, Karen!" Horrified reality bit her hard as she heard the front door open and heard Dad and Karen's husband, Brian, welcome the new visitor. "I can't believe this."

"Go wipe the flour off your face and brush your hair."

But it was too late. Brian escorted the poor, unsuspecting sucker into the kitchen.

"Victor's here, honey. He brought a fruitcake."

"How thoughtful," Karen gushed. "I'd like you to meet my sister, Esther."

Esther unconsciously swiped at the flour on her face that Karen had mentioned, with no idea whether she actually removed it or not. Victor towered over her and his brown eyes were kind. He smiled, extending his hand.

"Very nice to meet you, Esther. Your sister sings your praise."

"Well, she's said some nice things about you, too."

"Can I take your coat?" Karen's voice intruded upon the niceties.

Victor shrugged out of a sheepskin coat, revealing a neatly cut outfit of dress slacks and a shirt and tie.

"I'll go put this away. You two get acquainted."

"I'm afraid I'm a little overdressed," he said, glancing at his clothes with a sheepish grin.

"Oh?" Then she nodded as understanding dawned. "Dad and Brian are Neanderthals. We can barely get them to dress up for church on Sunday mornings. Karen should have warned you the guys would be wearing jeans."

"I almost wore a suit coat. So at least I'm spared that humiliation in front of 'the guys.'"

Esther laughed. "It's pretty obvious why Karen wanted to fix us up."

His eyes took on a guarded look and Esther felt her cheeks warm.

"I mean, we both have a sense of humor."

He pasted a polite smile on his face, and Esther could feel him tense. With a heavy sigh, she realized she was making things worse. Better just to come out and say it.

"What I'm trying to tell you is that I'm in love with the man I was engaged to marry," she blurted. "I'm not ready to date anyone else."

He looked so relieved, Esther felt a bit insulted.

"The truth of the matter is that I'm engaged to be married."

"You are?"

"Yes. We haven't told anyone yet. Her parents won't like the fact that she's moving here from New York, and I wanted to get money saved and buy our home so there would be that much less they have to worry about."

"Congratulations," Esther said, feeling the tension drain from her.

"Congratulations about what?" Karen asked, as she breezed back into the kitchen.

"Victor was just telling me he's engaged to a girl back home."

Karen's disappointment was apparent. "Engaged? You didn't tell me that."

"I was afraid you might not invite me to dinner if I told you I was off the market."

Esther chortled. "Serves you right for trying to fix us up. I told you I wasn't ready to date again."

Karen grinned. "Well, at least I got a fruitcake out of it, even if I'm not getting a new brother-in-law."

During dinner, Esther tried to stay in the conversation, but her thoughts transported her to Tom and his family. Were they watching a football game? Most likely. And laughing and joking as they always did.

How did little Tommy look in his first Christmas outfit?

And Tom. What was he thinking at this moment?

Today would have been perfect if only they had stayed together and kept their plans. Right now, she'd be celebrating her first Christmas as Mrs. Pearson.

She excused herself from the table, went to the rest room, and cried.

fourteen

Tom couldn't help but smile at his six-month-old grandson, who sat in his stroller, enjoying the new warmth of early spring. His chubby fingers were wrapped around a teething ring, and he chewed voraciously, pausing occasionally to blow bubbles between his rosebud lips.

Due to an attack of spring fever, Ashley had decided to dive into cleaning every nook and cranny of her apartment and had recruited Trevor, Chris, and Minnie's help to accomplish the task. That left Tom with baby-sitting duty. Not that he minded. He couldn't get enough of the little guy.

"Tom?"

The familiar voice sent his heart into overdrive. He glanced up to find Esther staring down at him, her look of bewilderment matching the way he felt at the coincidence. "Esther. This is a pleasant surprise."

"Yes, it is." She glanced at Tommy. "Where's Ashley?"

Tom's heart sank. Was she disappointed to see him? It had been months since they'd even exchanged an e-mail. He missed her so badly at times, it was all he could do not to pick up the phone and ask her to dinner. But that wouldn't be fair to either of them. So, during those moments of weakness, he prayed for strength and wisdom. He had to admit, breaking up with Esther had done wonders for his relationship with God. And he didn't regret that for a second. He did, however, regret the way things had turned out.

"She roped everyone but me into spring cleaning."

Amusement twitched her beautiful, full lips. Tom swallowed hard and forced his gaze back to Tommy.

"Well," she said, plopping onto the bench next to him. "Looks like we've been duped."

"What do you mean?" He drank deeply of her flowery scent, like a man dying of thirst.

"Ashley called and asked if I'd like to bring the kids to the park since it's such a beautiful day."

He threw back his head and laughed, feeling happier than he had in months. "My daughter is quite the matchmaker, isn't she? I wondered how she talked Minnie and Chris into helping her clean. They must have banded together."

"And used three innocent children to accomplish their plot."

"You brought the kids?"

She gave him a teasing smile. "Would I come to the park without them? They're playing over there." She motioned toward the sandbox.

Tom smiled as the little girl dumped a shovel full of sand over the little boy's head. The boy stood, shook off, and sat back down without so much as yelling at her.

"Wow. He's a patient little tyke, isn't he? When my kids were that age, they would have been screaming for me to do something."

"Chuck practically raised her until they came to live with me. The only time he gets impatient is when she forgets her manners or does something he's afraid she'll get into trouble for." She leaned in and gave him a conspiratorial grin. "Not that she ever even comes close to getting into trouble."

She spoke of those children with emotion—just like every other mother he'd ever encountered. Joy mixed with pride—a recipe that exuded from her. Her smile seemed wider and even more genuine than he remembered. It didn't matter that these children weren't her flesh and blood. It was obvious that her love was fierce and real.

He couldn't help but smile. "Motherhood seems to agree with you."

She nodded. "It's wonderful. Much more than I ever dreamed, really."

Tom's gaze rested fondly on her. Indeed, she glowed like a woman about to give birth. Her eyes shone with love as she looked at the children playing in the sandbox. She'd put on a few pounds, he observed, but the extra padding did nothing to diminish her beauty. In fact, it gave her a softer look, which he found extremely appealing—too appealing.

"How long will these two be with you?"

She breathed a sigh and fixed her troubled gaze upon him. Her obvious anxiety shot straight to his heart.

"What's wrong?" he asked.

"To tell you the truth, I'm trying to adopt them. But I'm afraid it might not materialize."

Tom couldn't quite analyze the emotions flooding him. Somewhere in his heart, he supposed, he'd hoped she'd keep the kids until it was time for them to leave and then she'd be satisfied and ready to settle into the rest of her life with him. Now he saw the idiocy and selfishness of such presumption. And he saw how badly it would hurt her if she were to lose those children. "What's the problem?"

"Their mother is in prison for drugs. She keeps waffling back and forth about signing away her parental rights."

"Sounds like she's not ready to give them up. Could she get help and be fit to parent?" As soon as Tom spoke the words, he wished he could take them back. She'd confided in him as a friend needing support. She didn't need to hear the other side of the story when she was already hurting. Her scowl testified to that fact.

Before he could find his voice and apologize, she launched

her side of the equation like a rocket. Straightforward and to the point.

"She left Chuck in charge of Tonya for days at a time. A five year old! In my opinion, a woman like that doesn't deserve children."

"And yet God gave them to her." Tom cringed. What was his problem? This was not the way to win friends and influence people.

She sniffed. "Maybe God gave them to her because He knew I'd never find a man and wouldn't have any of my own. Don't you think it's possible He allowed her to have children so that I can have them?"

Stung and feeling the brunt of her verbal attack and implication, Tom averted his gaze to his grandson, who had dropped off to sleep.

"Oh, Tom. I'm sorry. I don't mean to sound so bitter. I really do understand why you wouldn't want to start a whole new family." Tears formed in her eyes. "I just can't stand the thought of losing those children. They love me, and I love them."

At the sound of fear in her voice, Tom finally caved and put his arm around her. She buried her face in his neck, accepting the comfort he offered. He whispered against her ear the words he felt God wanted him to speak. "God has a perfect plan for you, Esther. You need to know that, even if Chuck and Tonya go back to their mother."

"I can't imagine why God would allow that," she mumbled. He could feel her tears on his neck. "It makes no sense to me."

"God's ways often make little sense to us, sweetheart. His ways are higher, His thoughts higher. But if we put ourselves into His hands, He makes our lives a work of art that He, the Master Craftsman, creates."

He heard his words, but applying them to his own life hadn't been so easy. Coming to the park alone with Tommy had brought back all the memories of bringing up his kids alone. No one to sit with and share the funny things they did that day. No one to share in the load. When he'd married his wife, they'd never dreamed that he would be raising their children alone. But he had. It hadn't always felt like God working and molding his life. Mostly it had been a lot of hard work. Although, if he were honest, he'd have to admit there were a lot of happy times, too.

Esther shuddered in his arms, pulling Tom back to the present. Tom's throat tightened. He pulled her back and looked her in the eyes. Tears stained her cheeks. He reached into the diaper bag at the back of the stroller and grabbed a Kleenex.

Taking the tissue, she swiped at her eyes and nose, then gathered a shaky breath.

"Thanks."

"You're welcome." He turned to look at the children she'd taken into her heart. They played contentedly, happily, as children should, without the worries their short lives had brought them. Would God allow them to go back to the woman who had neglected them? If so, what would that do to the woman he loved? He turned and caught the full force of her gaze, questioning, loving. He bit back the words "I love you." But he could feel himself weaken.

She broke their gaze and turned back to the children. For the first time, Tom could imagine his life in their house. . .the one that had just been completed. Only now he could see the swing set in the backyard, bikes on the porch, and a basketball goal over the garage.

What was happening to him?

❧

"Okay, you need a bath, little boy." Esther glanced fondly at Chuck, who had tried to brush the sand from his clothes, but with little success. Her arms ached from the weight of

Tonya's sleeping body. "Head in there and strip out of those clothes while I lay Tonya down. I'll be in to run your water in a sec."

"Tonya's going to get the bed dirty," Chuck observed, his little face twisted into a scowl.

"I'll clean it up later. I promise."

Apparently satisfied, the boy headed to the bathroom to do as he'd been instructed.

Esther laid the toddler on the burgundy-striped comforter and sat at the edge of the bed to remove the little girl's shoes. One baby-plump cheek was red from where it had rested against Esther's shoulder, and her hair was damp from sweat. Esther wanted to curl up next to the child, to feel her warmth and smell her baby scent. To hold onto these precious times that she feared may not last forever.

The phone rang and she jumped, her stomach knotting as it did every time she got a call. That familiar sense of dread that Karen was calling to tell her the children's mother had made a final decision not to sign never failed to cause a rush of adrenaline.

She hurried to the phone and sucked in a breath at Tom's name on the caller ID.

"Hello?"

"Hi. It's—um—Tom."

"I know," she said, aware her voice sounded as breathless as she felt. Seeing him at the park had been a dream come true—the familiar dream. Meeting by chance. Tom taking her into his arms and telling her he still loved her. Today hadn't been quite like that. She'd snapped at him, then blubbered all over him. And now he was calling her?

"I know this is going to seem odd, but I wonder if you'd mind letting me take you and the kids out for pizza?"

Managing to stifle a gasp, she clutched the phone tighter.

"I don't understand. Are you asking us on a date? Or do you feel sorry for me?"

"I—" He hesitated, and she held her breath until he continued. "—guess I'm asking you on a date."

"I don't know what to say. You know I haven't changed my mind?"

"I know. And I can't say I've completely changed mine, but I have to tell you, Esther, I can't stop thinking about you. Life without you has made me very unhappy."

"Oh, Tom. Same for me." Her legs felt like rubber, and she sank to the couch next to the phone charger. "Seeing you again today was wonderful. But. . ."

"I know. You haven't changed your position on wanting children. I have to say, I don't know how I feel anymore, but I would like to at least explore the possibility."

Speechless, Esther stared at the opposite wall.

"Esther?"

"Yes. I'm here."

"I know it's a little unfair of me to ask you this when I'm not sure if I'll bale out again."

Her heart sank. Could she go through another breakup? "What exactly are you proposing?"

"I'd like to spend time with you and the kids. Casually. I promise I'll keep my hands to myself."

She smiled into the empty room.

"So what do you think?"

"Pizza sounds good. Give me an hour at least to finish bathing the kids and get myself ready."

"Okay, I'll see you in an hour."

Esther's heart sang a happy tune as she went about her routine, readying herself and the children for the date.

It couldn't be a coincidence that Tom was coming back at this time. This was everything she'd prayed for—everything she'd told God she wanted. Maybe she was finally about to get everything she'd longed for. Tom and the children would make her life complete.

❧

Chuck was nothing at all like Chris had been at nearly six years old. Tom watched the sensitive child with growing admiration. His table manners were impeccable. He didn't ask for a thing but never forgot to say "thank you" to the waitress who delivered the drinks and pizza or to Esther for handing him a slice. Where Chris continually had to be told to wipe his mouth, Chuck wiped his own and his sister's as well.

They would never have to worry about this kid embarrassing them in public. He allowed his attention to focus on Esther. She caught his gaze, and he realized she'd been watching him watch the kids. Her expression was tender as her lips curved—tender and a bit confident. He returned her smile. Perhaps she had good reason to be confident.

"Would you care to take a drive after dinner?" he asked.

Her brow rose. "Where to?"

"Can I surprise you?"

Lips twitching, she studied him for a second, then nodded.

"Well, look who's here." Tom turned to find Minnie and Mitch walking up to the table.

"Minnie!" The two women embraced. Then Esther reached out and gave Mitch a quick hug as well.

"You look amazing!" Esther said.

"Thanks. I have you to thank for encouraging me to go to the gym."

"You had to do the work. I can't believe the difference."

"I think she looked great before she lost all the weight."

At Mitch's remark, Esther and Minnie exchanged grins, and Tom had the feeling he was being left out of a private conversation.

"Are you going to join us?" Esther asked.

Minnie turned to Mitch. "You want to?"

"Sure." He grinned and stood back while Minnie slid into the booth ahead of him.

Esther's pleasure at seeing the two of them worked magic on Tom's mood, and he found himself glad that they'd stopped by.

"So, how are ya, Chuckie?" Minnie asked the little guy.

"Good." He blushed and looked away. But that didn't deter Minnie.

"So, what have you been doing this week?"

He shrugged. "Playing." His eyes brightened. "Me and Tonya played at the park today."

"Oh, really?" Minnie tossed Tom a saucy grin. "My dad played at the park today, too, didn't he?"

Chuck glanced nervously at Tom, but obviously catching the teasing spirit of the moment, he giggled and nodded. Minnie ruffled his hair. "You fit in just fine, sport."

Before Tom could do damage control to that statement, she switched her focus to Esther. "I haven't seen you at the gym in a few weeks, Esther."

Esther grimaced. "I know. I need to get back, but I've been swamped with last-minute tax filers and the kids. Certain things have had to get put on the back burner."

So that explained the extra pounds. Tom filed away the information. Perhaps he could relieve her a couple of times a week so she could hit the gym if she wanted to.

"So what are you two doing out?" she asked, her gaze darting to Mitch, then back to Minnie.

Minnie shrugged. "Just hanging out."

"Ha. It's a date," Mitch countered. "She's embarrassed to admit I finally wore her down."

Tom stifled a disbelieving laugh just as he noticed his

daughter's cheeks brighten. "A date?" he said, unable to keep the incredulity from his voice.

Esther let out a short almost imperceptible laugh. "I have a feeling I'll be getting an apology over the radio."

Remembering his bold promise to apologize and dedicate a song to her when Minnie and Mitch announced their engagement, Tom added his amusement to hers.

"What's that supposed to mean?" Minnie asked, her voice suspicious.

"Oh, nothing."

"So have you gone out to see the house yet?" Mitch asked.

His face twisted with pain, leaving Tom to assume Minnie had kicked him under the table.

"What house?" Esther asked.

No sense in lying to her or keeping her in the dark. "Ours." Tom hoped the longing he felt rising in his heart didn't disclose itself in the tone of his voice.

"Our house is finished?" Her gaze fixed on his. He loved the way "our house" rolled from her lips as though they were still an *us*.

He nodded and the rest of the world fell away as he became captured in the depths of her amber-colored eyes.

"Is that where you were going to take me tonight after dinner?"

"Yes."

"I'm dying to see it."

"Then let's go."

fifteen

Esther said a hurried good-bye to Tom at the door. The journey they had taken out to the house that they'd planned to share had been an emotional one. And now that they were back at Esther's house, they both realized it would be best if she went inside alone. No sense in giving place to the devil. Or making it more painful if they didn't end up back together.

The phone was ringing by the time Esther and the children made it inside. "Chuck, honey, go brush your teeth and put on your pajamas." She set Tonya down, and the little girl toddled after her brother as Esther snatched up the phone.

"I've been trying to call all evening," Karen snapped at the other end of the line. "Why didn't you have your cell on?"

"Hey, Kare," she said. "Sorry. I forgot to grab my phone on the way out earlier. The kids and I were with Tom. He took us to see our house." She grinned, expecting her sister to pounce on the comment.

Instead, a nervous cough came over the line. "Listen, I have something to tell you," Karen said, her troubled tone searing into Esther's consciousness. She sat, bracing herself for the news she was almost certain was forthcoming.

"What's wrong? Their mother won't give in?"

"It's worse than that."

"What?" Her sense of foreboding caused nausea to rise in her stomach. What could be worse than that? "Tell me."

"I don't know how to say this."

Esther heard her slow intake of breath.

"Say it." The tears spilled over before Karen even spoke.

"It seems as though Chuck and Tonya's mother has family out there after all."

"What do you mean?"

"She has parents."

"What kind of parents let their daughter sit in jail while her kids go to foster care?" Esther tried to process the information amid rising fear and anger. Not an easy task to accomplish and remain reasonable. But she didn't care. If Karen was going where it seemed she was going, Esther didn't want to be reasonable. She refused to be reasonable. She couldn't bear what was coming with a logical mind.

Karen's voice broke as she continued. "Apparently the children's mother ran away from home when she found out she was pregnant with Chuck. She and her parents never got along, and she was afraid to tell them. So she left with her boyfriend instead, who of course didn't stick around very long. She recently contacted her parents and they've reconciled. They want the children, and she's signed over custody to them."

Panic rose hot and fast inside Esther, tightening her throat and causing her words to come out in a hoarse near-scream. "That's not possible! They can't have them."

"Esther, you need to pull yourself together and think about this. Chuck and Tonya have grandparents who love them, sight unseen, and want to provide a loving home. We can't deny them or the children the basic right to be with family."

"How loving can they be if their own daughter ran away from home rather than telling them she was pregnant? What if they hit her?" The thought of Chuck and Tonya going into an abusive home nearly sent her running to her bedroom for suitcases. She'd run away with them before allowing them to be harmed.

"Esther, I've met them. I don't believe they're a threat to the children."

"You met them without telling me first?" The sense of betrayal she felt overshadowed any pain she'd ever dealt with.

"I didn't want to worry you unnecessarily," Karen replied, with no hint of apology. "And after meeting them, I have no good reason for keeping those children from their grandparents."

Reason invaded her fortress of emotion. Her hand trembled as she brought it up to swipe at the tears coursing down her cheeks. "H—how long do I have with them?"

"Just tonight."

"So soon?" She searched for an answer, anything that might buy her some time. "Couldn't we have a few visits with them so the children can get to know their grandparents first?"

"That's not the way things are done in cases like this one."

"Karen, what about God? How can we let them go to people who may not be Christians?" She grasped at this. Surely, God wouldn't send the children into a godless home. "Chuck loves his classes at church, and he's learning so much."

"Esther, please. Stop tormenting yourself." She hesitated. "I'll tell you this much. Their grandmother said, 'Praise the Lord,' when I told her how safe and well cared for the children have been over the past few months. So, I imagine they are Christians. I know it's hard, but you're going to have to deal with this."

"B—but what if they're scared? They don't know these people."

"They didn't know you either when they came to live with you." Karen's voice remained even, and Esther recognized the tone her sister used when trying to calm the people she dealt with on a daily basis. The knowledge made her uneasy and embarrassed her to think she had to be "dealt with."

She forced herself to calm down. "All right. When are you picking them up?"

"In the morning. On my way to the office."

"I'll have their things packed and ready to go."

"I know this is difficult for you, but the pain will pass. I promise."

"You have a husband and three beautiful children that no one can take away from you." Esther knew she was being unfair, but how much more must she lose before God decided it was time to let her win? "You have no idea how I feel."

She dropped the phone into the cradle without saying good-bye. But she didn't care. Karen was obviously not on her side in this.

Chuck's voice calling from the other room pulled her from the veil of bitterness. "Mom? I have my jammies on. Will you read me a story now?"

Mom. Chuck had been calling her that for the past week. Only one short week to bear that wonderful title. *Oh, God. It's not fair!*

⁂

Tom's heart raced as he sped along Highway 51 toward the "house." Esther had been hysterical when she called. Even in her worst moments, he'd never seen her be more than a little nervous or upset.

The memory of her voice on the phone a few minutes earlier caused him to press the accelerator.

"Tom, can you meet me at the house?" she'd asked.

"Esther? Honey, what's wrong?"

"Please. Can you meet me?"

He'd pulled on his clothes and had made it to his truck in less than five minutes.

She was standing beside her car when he pulled up behind her.

He left the motor running and the lights on as he hopped out of the truck and hurried to her. In the glow from the headlights, he saw her face, red and swollen from crying. Her hair was tousled and her eyes wild with anxiety.

"Baby, what's wrong? Did something happen to the kids?"

She shook her head and motioned toward the car. He peered in through the window. Both children were sleeping peacefully in the backseat.

"Tell me what happened."

Sobbing, she fell into his arms. For several minutes, he held her. Each time it appeared she was pulling herself together and would tell him what was wrong, the tears began anew.

Finally, he gripped her arms and pulled her away from him. He studied her ashen face. "What's the matter?"

"They're taking the kids away."

"Who?"

"Karen."

"Your sister is taking Chuck and Tonya? Why?"

She gulped and swiped at her face with her sleeve. The childlike action slammed into his heart.

"Their grandparents have been located."

"I'm sorry, honey. So sorry."

She clutched at his shirt. "Will you help me?"

"Help you what?"

"I—I want to run away. Take the kids and just go to Mexico or. . .or Canada. Someplace where they can't find us."

Horror gripped Tom's heart. "Are you crazy?"

She pounded his chest with her fists. Tom took hold of her wrists and gently pulled her back.

"I can't lose those kids! They're mine, Tom. Th—they call me Mom. They love *me*."

The determination in her face sent a shudder of fear through him. Who was this woman?

"Esther. You can't run away with them. Do you want to go to prison?"

"I won't get caught."

"Honey, you *will* get caught. And when Chuck thinks of you years from now, he'll only remember the woman who ran away with him and his sister. Is that how you want to be remembered?"

She stopped struggling and looked up at him with such grief, it was all he could do not to pack her and the kids up and do as she wanted. Anything to ease her pain. He pulled her to him and stroked her hair. "Let Chuck and Tonya remember you as the woman who took them in and loved them until they went to live with their grandparents."

She wilted against him as though she had no more fight left in her. Tom lost track of time as she sobbed quietly in his arms.

"Come on. Let's go back to your house so the kids can go to bed."

She nodded and didn't protest when he settled her into the passenger side of her car. "I'm going to move my truck out of the way and then I'm driving you home."

By the time they arrived at her house, Esther had stopped crying, and she stared sullenly out the window. Tom glanced in the backseat. The children never even awoke during the ordeal.

"I'll carry Chuck in. Can you get the baby, or should I come back for her?"

"I'll get her," she said dully.

"Is your door locked?"

"The key's on the keychain in the ignition."

Tom took the keys and slid out of the car. He opened the

back door and carefully pulled Chuck out. After he opened the door, he waited for Esther to precede him and then followed her inside.

She led him into the children's bedroom, where she deposited the little girl, kissed her cheek, and waited for Tom to lay Chuck down so she could kiss him, too.

He heard a sharp intake of breath and knew the tears were coming again.

"Come on," he said softly. He took her gently by the arm. "Let's go into the living room."

Dropping onto the gray overstuffed couch, she covered her face with her hands. "What am I going to do without those kids?"

Sitting next to her, he slid his arm along the back of the couch and rubbed her shoulder as she leaned her head back against him. "You'll make it, sweetheart."

"Don't you see? Chuck and Tonya were my future. After you and I broke up, I realized I'd never have children. But God immediately brought those two into my life. It was like He was saying, 'I closed one door, but look, here's an open door. All you have to do is walk through it.'"

Tom swallowed hard. He continued to rub her shoulder. "He didn't close that door, Esther. I did."

Her silky hair brushed against his arm as she turned to face him. "Either way, it closed."

"This evening when we had the kids out for pizza, I could see myself raising them. I could see us together as a family."

Her eyes filled with tears again. "That would have been wonderful."

He wanted to say so much more, but he sensed now wouldn't be a good time. She was vulnerable and so was he. "I'm going to call Minnie to come over and stay with you tonight. I don't want you to be alone."

He reached over her to take the phone. She clutched his shirt as he hovered over her, balancing so that he didn't fall on her. He glanced down into her amber-colored eyes—those expressive eyes that said so much. Replacing the phone, he gathered her in his arms, taking her lips with his, exploring the passion he'd denied them both for half a year. She matched him kiss for kiss, pressing closer, tempting his control until he finally pulled away and stood. He turned away, unable to look at her mussed hair, her kiss-swollen lips. "We need to stop."

"Why?"

She rose and wrapped her arms around him from behind. He sent a silent prayer to heaven.

"Why? Because neither of us wants to sin, that's why."

"You still love me, don't you?" Esther's breath was warm on his back through his T-shirt. "Aren't we on the way to getting back together?"

He turned and her arms slid around his neck. "I'd like to think so. But you're not thinking straight."

"I missed you so much." She leaned closer and Tom's senses buzzed. "I just want to be in your arms. Is there anything wrong with that? We're getting married anyway."

He sucked in a quick breath. He'd hoped she wasn't suggesting they be intimate. He'd hoped she only needed his arms around her. To be close. But there was no mistaking her meaning. Taking her wrists, he pulled her away from him. "Honey, if we were married, I could hold you all night and try to comfort you, but we're not. I can't take you trying to seduce me. I love you and want you too much, and no matter how badly you're hurting or how mad you are at God, you can't justify sin."

Tears slid down her cheeks. "Oh, Tom. I'm sorry for throwing myself at you that way. Of course I don't want to sin. I just—I can't bear this. It feels like my heart is being ripped from my body."

Mercy replaced desire. Kindness replaced passion. He gathered her to him. "It'll be all right." He pressed a kiss to her temple. "I'm going to call Minnie, now."

Thankfully, Minnie was still awake and agreed to come right away. Esther sat on the couch, hugging a throw pillow. She barely spoke during the thirty minutes it took for Minnie to arrive.

Tom bent down and kissed her head. "I love you, honey. I'll be back in the morning."

Minnie walked him to the door.

"Thank you for coming, sweetheart," he said, brushing his lips against her cheek, which now clearly showed cheekbones.

"I don't mind, Dad. Just make sure you tell Mitch where I am if he calls."

"So Greg's history, huh?"

"Oh, yeah."

"I'm happy for you. Mitch is a great guy."

"Yeah, you'd think I'd have figured that out sooner." She glanced back at Esther. "What about you two?"

"I'm praying things will work out."

"So you might want to have more kids?"

Not exactly the conversation he'd have chosen to have with his daughter, but he guessed she deserved an answer. "I would have raised Chuck and Tonya, so I guess I am softening." He grinned. "Maybe Chris will get his wish for a baby brother or sister after all."

Minnie bit her bottom lip as she did when she was nervous.

"What?"

"I don't think Esther's going to have an easy time getting over those two. Go easy suggesting more kids."

"When did you grow up?" he asked, unable to keep the admiration from his tone.

"About the time Esther came into our lives. I hope we can keep her this time."

"Me, too, sweetie. Me, too."

sixteen

Thick clouds of despair settled over Esther from the moment Karen's car had pulled away carrying the children. Now, two weeks later, she couldn't pull herself together long enough to do simple tasks. The phone rang, and she ignored it. The doorbell chimed, and she pretended she wasn't home, though anyone could see her car in the driveway. But she didn't care. Her reason for living was gone.

She knew she was in a heavy depression, but she was powerless against it. She tried to read her Bible, but the words were empty. The life she used to draw from the weatherworn pages was gone, and she read familiar passages with a sense of boredom.

She tried to watch TV, but nothing appealed to her. So she kept it on for the noise, but found no pleasure in the mindless jokes that usually entertained her. Books held no appeal, either, and she stayed away from church. How could she sit on those padded chairs and pretend everything was all right when she was facing the darkest time in her life? From her years of knowing God, she was cognizant of the fact that only He could pull her through this. But she lacked the willpower to allow Him to do so. Not yet.

The doorbell chimed. She ignored it. It chimed again. She ignored it again. The persistent visitor banged on the door. Finally, curiosity got the best of her, and she glanced out the window. With a groan, she recognized Karen's minivan. After a few more minutes of banging, Esther got the message that her sister was not going away. With a heavy sigh, she pulled herself from her bed and shuffled into the living room. "I'm not really up to company, Karen," she called through the door.

"Too bad. I'm not leaving until you open up."

"Fine," she groused. She unlocked the door. "It's open."

"Unlock the storm door so I can come in." The determination in Karen's eyes told Esther it was useless to argue.

She flicked the lock. "Okay. Come in."

Karen took one look at her, and her eyes filled with tears. "Oh, Esther." Without an invitation, she put her arms around Esther. "I'm so sorry you're hurting."

Pulling away, Esther went to the couch and plopped down. "Yeah, well." She wanted to say hateful things. Wanted to tell her sister she could have prevented them from taking away Chuck and Tonya, but she knew that wasn't fair. Even through the pain and depression, she wasn't so far gone that she couldn't control her hateful tongue.

"When was the last time you ate?" Karen asked.

Esther thought about it and shrugged. "Yesterday, I think."

"Look at you. You're skin and bones. Go take a shower and get dressed. I'm taking you out for lunch."

"No way. I don't want to be around people."

"Too bad. Go take a shower, or I'm going to carry you, even if I have to call for reinforcements from the other people who love you."

"You wouldn't get much help. It's a short list."

Karen studied her for a minute, then took a deep breath. "It's your own fault for telling Tom to get lost."

"Hey, I thought you were here to console me."

"You thought wrong." Karen placed her hands on her hips. "I'm here to help you snap out of this depression. But, I think this is more than just depression over the kids. It's gone on too long, Esther."

"What do you mean? What else is there?"

"Maybe it's due to perimenopause. I think you should call your doctor again."

"Give me a break."

"Think about it. This isn't like you. You've always rolled with the punches. Even when it looked like you would lose the business a couple of years ago. Remember? When Mom died, you took control and got everyone else through it. This just isn't like you."

She hated the possibility that she couldn't control her emotions because of a freak of raging hormones. Anger shot through her at the thought. On the other hand, if that were the problem, it would mean she wasn't going crazy. That she could get a grip on life again. Could function. Work. Love. Tom. . .

"Do you really think that's what all this is about?" Somehow, it felt like she wasn't properly grieving over the kids if the depression was due to hormonal levels.

"I think this, on top of losing Tom and the kids, was too much. But your doctor will be able to tell you more about that than I can. Will you see her?"

Knowing she couldn't go on much longer in this state, Esther nodded. "All right, I'll call her."

❧

Tom had to make a fist to keep from picking up the phone and calling Esther.

"Believe me, Tom, I'm not the woman for you," she'd said to him last time they'd spoken—the day the children had left her home.

He'd thought she'd be ecstatic with the news that he'd be willing to have a child if it would make her happy. Instead, she'd asked him to leave—had told him obviously God had decided she wasn't fit to be a mother. As much as he'd tried to figure it all out over the past four weeks, the answers eluded him. Her partner was taking care of all Esther's accounts for the time being, so he couldn't even pretend he needed to talk business with her. E-mails bounced back as though her inbox was too full.

"What more does she want?" he growled at the silent phone.

"You okay, Dad?"

Heat crawled up his neck as Chris walked into the kitchen. The boy gave him a curious look and continued across the room to grab a bowl and the cereal. "So, no luck with Esther, huh?" he asked with all the sensitivity of a high-school kid.

"No."

"Sorry, Dad. I really liked her a lot."

Tom smiled at his son. "Thanks. So did I. Loved her, in fact. Still do."

"Can't you tell her that? Maybe she'll change her mind. I mean, she was going to marry you. She must have loved you."

Releasing a heavy breath, Tom realized this is what he'd sunk to—pouring out his heart to his teenaged son. But knowing how pathetic that was didn't deter him from opening his mouth. "I know she loves me. But losing those two foster kids really broke her heart."

Chris spooned a mound of Chocolate Dots into his mouth. "Well, maybe you ought to change your mind about having a kid."

Tom grimaced and fought the urge to tell him not to talk with his mouth full. When did kids outgrow that tendency?

"Believe me, I'm willing to have a kid if it'll make her happy. Anything to convince her to marry me."

"Well, I hope you didn't tell her *that*." Minnie appeared from the hallway. His life was an open book. She strolled to the refrigerator, grabbed a string cheese stick, and plopped into a chair across from Tom. She glanced at Chris and scowled. "Do you know how many carbs are in that junk?"

He grabbed the box, took a look at the nutritional information, and glanced back at her. "Yep." He shoveled another spoonful into his mouth.

Minnie rolled her eyes. "So, Dad, you decided you'd have a baby with Esther? Have you told her?"

Averting his gaze to the table, he nodded. "I told her." But after Minnie's outburst, he realized he'd been less than gracious about it. "But I think I might have goofed."

A groan escaped Minnie's lips.

"I think she might have gotten the impression that I was willing to have a baby as a favor to her rather than it being something I want, too."

Her brow rose and Chris stopped crunching. Both stared, disbelief written across their faces.

"You mean you actually *want* to have a baby?" Minnie asked. "You weren't just giving in so Esther will marry you?"

"At first I think it was about giving in. But after I saw her with Chuck and Tonya, I could honestly see the two of us raising kids together."

"Wow. That's quite a change of heart."

Minnie's scrutiny forced the truth from him, a truth he'd known in his heart but refused to acknowledge in words. "It's been tough raising you three kids alone. There were nights I fell into bed for two or three hours of sleep before I had to get up and start another day."

"You did a great job, Dad."

"Thanks. But I was a young man back then. Still full of energy." He gave them a wry grin. "I'm not so young anymore. The thought of having a baby and then losing Esther sent me into a tailspin."

"And what changed your mind?"

"Well, mostly God. I know I'm not alone. If, God forbid, I lost another wife and found myself alone again, I have three adult children to help me."

"Hey, don't expect me to change a diaper!" Chris said, coming up for air from his second bowl of cereal.

"Don't talk with your mouth full, spaz."

Tom grinned. Oh, yeah. A lot of help they'd be. Bottom line was that he had to somehow convince Esther that his objections weren't out of selfishness, but out of fear—and that God had helped him deal with that fear.

seventeen

Esther knew she should return Tom's persistent calls, but the truth of the matter was that he'd made her mad and she wasn't quite ready to let go of her anger. The last thing she'd wanted to hear the day she'd lost the children was Tom's self-sacrificing statement, and even now that she was feeling better, she was still ticked off.

The temptation to pick up the phone and tell him exactly why he'd said the wrong thing was strong from time to time. But she didn't know how to make him understand that she didn't want his *willingness* to have a baby, but his *desire* to have one. How did she explain that if he didn't truly want a child, then she'd always feel as though she'd forced him into it? She would always be insecure in the relationship and afraid that he resented her for essentially giving him an ultimatum—agree to give me a child within X amount of time or you can't have me.

She glanced over at the phone and quickly returned her attention to the account on her computer. Today was her first day back at work, and she had a ton to do. If she worked fifteen-hour days for the next month, she still wouldn't be caught up.

A knock at her door pulled her attention away from her stress-filled thoughts. Heaving a sigh, she called, "Come in." Just what she needed—another distraction.

Missy stood at the door, her face hidden behind a huge bouquet of mixed flowers. "You are one lucky woman," she said, stepping in and setting the vase on Esther's desk. "Call the man back."

A smile played at the corners of Esther's lips. "Thanks, Missy." Unable to squelch the thrill shooting through her veins, she opened the card.

> *Tune in to FM 91.7 at 2 p.m. today.*
> *Tom*

Esther grinned. *Time to pay the piper.* Minnie and Mitch must have announced their engagement. She wouldn't miss this public apology for anything in the world.

A glance at the clock revealed she had thirty minutes to wait, so she forced herself to return to her task.

She sighed, rummaging through a sheaf of papers. The next time she asked a client for an income statement and balance sheet, she would specify that she was looking for more than a shoebox filled with a year's worth of bank statements and check stubs. There were a few receipts turned in for good measure. These people ate more pizza than anyone she'd ever known.

Making a mental note to recommend a software program that might work a little better than a cardboard box in keeping records, she dove into the clutter with gusto, separating receipts into two piles—tax-deductible and "You wish."

When Missy buzzed her sometime later, she barely even looked up as she pressed the button. "Yeah?"

"Your sister is on the line. Want to take it?"

A day at work wouldn't be normal, somehow, if Karen didn't interrupt something important. "I'll take it. Thanks."

She picked up the receiver and pushed the button for the right line. "Hey, Kare. What's going on?"

"Just checking up on you. Making sure you're not over-stressing yourself."

Esther chuckled. At least she was honest. "I'm doing all right. But the stress is pretty high. My desk is piled up. You wouldn't believe it. Seriously. This client—who shall remain nameless in the spirit of client confidentiality—is the worst organizer I've ever seen in my life. I'm telling you, Kare, I asked her to send me her record files from her software program so that I could just convert her files to mine and she laughed. Can you believe that?"

"Why'd she do that?" The lack of sympathy was more than evident, judging by the sound of Karen's amused laughter.

"She told me she uses cardboardware."

"Cardboardware? I've never heard of that."

"It's a shoebox."

Esther's comment was met with silence.

"Get it?" Esther pressed. "Cardboard? A shoebox?"

"Oh!" Karen started giggling. "I get it. That's kind of clever. Cardboardware."

Esther's frustration ebbed at the sound of Karen's laughter, and she found herself joining her sister. As they laughed, Esther's gaze traveled her desk until it lit on the vase of flowers. She gasped.

"What?" Karen said.

"What time is it?"

"Looks like about four minutes after two. Why?"

A groan escaped her. "I missed it!"

"What? What's wrong?"

"I have to go, Kare. I can't believe I missed it." Esther disconnected the call without saying good-bye. She flew to the radio. "Cardboardware," she muttered disgustedly as she pushed the scanner. It settled on the Christian radio station. She turned up the volume.

The DJ's voice blared through the speakers. "That was Tom. When a man admits he was wrong over the airwaves, you know he's in love. This song goes out to Esther from Tom. God bless you two."

Esther's heart sang along with the Christian love song. She would have given anything to have heard the announcement of Minnie's engagement, but this song proved that Tom still loved her. Her heart softened, and she let go of the anger she'd felt toward him. How could she blame a man if he didn't feel he wanted to start a whole new family after his children were already grown?

Strolling back to her desk chair, she allowed her thoughts to roam over the past couple of weeks. She'd made her appointment with the doctor and had blood tests. The results confirmed Karen's suspicions—she was suffering from a slight hormonal imbalance. Her doctor suggested a natural cream, absorbed through her skin, and suggested getting back into her exercise routine.

At first, Esther had been skeptical about the cream, but she had to admit, her life had come back into control when she started treatment. And aside from protesting muscles, it was great to be back at the gym four times a week.

She was feeling like her old self again—ready to rejoin life.

Chuck and Tonya were never far from her thoughts, but the searing pain she'd felt just weeks before was beginning to lessen with each new day. She'd resumed her daily devotions and the Word had begun to speak life to her sickly soul. Finally, the craziness and pain of loss had righted itself in her mind, and she was able to put things into perspective once again. . .to breathe in and out without feeling like every breath might be her last. Or wishing it would be.

The joy she felt at the flowers and the love song from Tom eased the aggravation of the poorly kept records of her client as she worked throughout the afternoon. She watched the phone from time to time, wondering if Tom would call.

After all, like the DJ said, when a man went on the radio to admit he was wrong, he must be in love.

By five-thirty, she realized he wasn't going to call. Had he decided that love wasn't enough to overcome all the obstacles they'd faced since meeting less than a year ago?

Maybe she should just cut her losses and move on. She'd lost the children and probably Tom. But at least she had her relationship with God and her sanity had returned. Maybe God was telling her that should be enough—to be content with the life He'd chosen for her.

&

Tom grabbed a mug from the shelf and closed the cabinet a little harder than he'd intended.

"I take it she didn't call." Minnie's accurate assumption ground into him like salt into a wound. He'd been watching the phone all day—ever since his radio debut. The female employees of the radio station had assured him that she'd race to the phone to call him. Boy, were they ever wrong.

"So maybe she wasn't listening to the radio."

"I made sure she'd tune in."

"I'm sorry, Dad."

He breathed a heavy sigh and plopped down onto a kitchen chair. "Me, too. I guess it's time to face facts. It's finally over for good."

&

Sweat rolled down Esther's cheeks as she finished her last mile on the treadmill. Reaching for her water, she switched the machine off, grabbed her towel, and stepped from the platform.

She headed to the locker room, stopping short at the sight of Minnie, lacing up gym shoes.

"Hey, Esther."

Was it her imagination or was the girl a little cool?

"Hi. This is a surprise."

A shrug lifted the girl's now slender shoulders. "Summer semester. My classes are all in the morning, so I have to work out in the afternoons for the next couple of months."

"So I guess congratulations are in order."

Minnie nodded. "Thanks. It's been a long time coming."

"I knew it would happen."

"Yeah. It was only a matter of time. I really applied myself the last few months. I know Dad's happy that I finally got it over with." She laughed.

Esther smiled. "Don't bet on it. Your dad's going to miss you. Mark my words."

"Oh, I'm staying home afterwards, so he won't really have a chance to miss me."

"You and Mitch are going to live with your dad?"

"Mitch? What's he got to do with it?"

Esther frowned. "Aren't you getting married?"

"Married? No way." Minnie's cheeks stained pink. "Well, someday, probably. But not now."

"Well, what did you think I was congratulating you for?"

"I'm graduating at the end of the summer instead of waiting for next year. I took a heavy course load last semester and decided to take summer classes. It's killing me, but it will be worth it to get on with my life." She frowned. "What did *you* think you were congratulating me for?"

It was Esther's turn to blush. Heat warmed her neck and cheeks. "I thought you were engaged to Mitch."

"Why would you think that?"

"Well, at your birthday barbeque, I noticed Mitch was crazy about you, but your dad insisted you two were just friends and always would be. So we made a deal that when Mitch proposed, your dad would go on the radio and admit he was wrong."

Minnie's eyes sparkled with amusement, and Esther could see she was fighting to keep from laughing outright.

"I know. It was pretty silly. But your dad went on the radio last week."

"Did you listen to that broadcast, Esther?"

"I missed the beginning," she admitted. "I caught the beautiful song he dedicated to me." Giving Minnie a sad smile, she forced back the sudden tears burning her eyes. "I thought he was sending me a message that he still loves me, but after a week without a call from him, I've gotten the message."

"What message?"

Esther was getting a little tired of Minnie's amusement. The girl might have the boy she loved, but that was no reason to be insensitive.

Gathering a steadying breath, she determined not to break down in front of Tom's daughter. "The song was obviously a farewell."

"If I'm not mistaken, he dedicated 'Our Love Will Last Forever.'"

"Yeah, that's it."

"That doesn't exactly sound like a farewell dedication to me."

"That's what I thought at first, too. I've been waiting for him to call, but I realized today he must have been saying that we'll always love each other even if we can't live together."

Minnie laughed outright. "Oh, Esther. This is priceless. Thank God He changed my schedule this semester."

"I don't mean to be uptight, Minnie, but this is really hurting me. I wish you wouldn't take it so lightly. Don't you remember how badly you felt when Greg didn't return your love?"

The girl sobered immediately. "I'm really sorry, Esther. But listen. You have this all wrong. Do you have plans right now?"

"I was going to shower, then go home and work some more."

"Will you come with me for a few minutes after you shower?"

"Where to?"

Minnie grinned. "Trust me?"

❧

"Tom, I really hope you're listening." Tom nearly wrecked at the sound of his name coming over the airwaves. He'd only been half listening to the DJ as he drove through rush-hour traffic. Even now, he wasn't positive he'd heard what he thought he had. He reached down and turned up the volume. Sure enough, the sweet voice on the radio belonged to Esther.

"Tom, I hope you're out there, buddy," the DJ said. "Because this beautiful lady has something to say to you."

"I–I just want to apologize for not calling you last week when you asked me to. I didn't know anything about it because I got distracted at work and missed the first few minutes."

Tom's heart beat a rapid rhythm in his chest. That explained a lot.

"So if you really meant what you said on the radio, meet me at the house. You know which one I mean."

"Okay," the DJ said, "I hope you two will connect this time. Keep us updated and God bless you. Tom, this is going out to you from Esther."

The strains of "Our Love Will Last Forever" floated through the truck. Tom made an illegal U-turn amid the blaring of two dozen horns. He hated to be the cause of more rush-hour stress for the other motorists, but he'd waited too long for this moment, and he wasn't about to miss out on his future.

❧

Esther pulled into the driveway half a minute ahead of Tom. He jumped out of his truck and was opening her car door before she could even kill the motor. He knelt in front of her, taking her hand. "I've missed you," he said and kissed her hand.

"Oh, Tom. I can't believe how crazy things have been the past few months. Can you ever forgive me?"

"Would I be here if I couldn't?" He tugged gently on her hand to help her from the car. "I need to ask your forgiveness, too."

"You? You've been so good throughout my craziness."

"Let's go up to the house."

Arm-in-arm, they walked toward the two-story gray brick dwelling.

"You've built such a beautiful home," Esther said, her eyes misting.

They sat on the porch swing. "Now," Tom said, taking her hand and lacing his fingers with hers. "The reason I need to apologize is this. That morning the children left, I said something really stupid."

"You mean about us having children?"

He nodded, and Esther's heart plummeted. But she wasn't willing to lose him no matter what.

"I understand. And Tom, I know you're the man God planned for me. He waited until just the right time in my life to bring us together. And, though I admit I want children, the most important person to me is you, and I'm sorry I put so much pressure on you."

He released her hand and slipped his arm around her shoulders, pulling her close until his face was poised an inch away. "Esther, I love you." Their breath mingled just before he covered her mouth with his.

As Esther slid her arms about his neck, she felt the gentle peace of knowing she was exactly where she was meant to be. In Tom's arms. She wasn't ready for him to pull away when he held her at arm's length a moment later.

"Now, I need to tell you something," he said. "When I apologized, I meant for acting like I was doing you a favor by agreeing to have a baby. The truth is, I was disappointed when Chuck and Tonya went to live with their grandparents. I was really starting to like the idea of marrying you and adopting them."

Tears formed in Esther's eyes and pain clutched her heart at the reminder of what might have been. "That would have been so wonderful. But I'm learning to submit to God's will, and I'm satisfied that Chuck and Tonya were never supposed to be my children."

"That's quite a revelation." Pride shone in his eyes, and joy rippled through Esther at his approval.

She nodded. "All my life, I've done things my way. I planned a path where I'd get my business going well, then I'd get married and have a child. There was no room for God to have His way because I didn't ask His advice. I kept waiting for God to change your mind so that you'd want to have a baby with me after our marriage. Instead, God showed me that His ways are perfect, and I'll be happiest when I learn to walk in His will."

"And if I want to have a child?"

She hadn't expected that option. "I'm through asking you for something you don't want as much as I do."

"I want us to raise a child together." He gazed so intently into her eyes that Esther couldn't deny his sincerity. "After Chuck and Tonya, I realized my hesitance wasn't due to not being ready to walk into my golden years with you, but fear that something might happen to you and I'd be forced to raise another child alone."

Esther drew a sharp breath. "I never even thought about that."

He nodded. "God's given me peace. And to be honest, I'm looking forward to going through the process with you."

Excitement rose and then crashed. "Oh, Tom. I have to tell you something."

Concern creased his brow. "What is it, sweetheart?"

She explained the doctor's concern about perimenopause.

Tears were flowing by the time she finished. Tom brushed a gentle kiss against her temple. "If I'm not mistaken, what you're telling me is that it's unlikely you'll get pregnant without a lot of help, but not impossible."

She nodded.

"Can you trust me to just take it one day at a time? We'll pray for God's will and let nature take its course."

She nodded.

He reached into his front pocket and pulled the familiar black box. With a sheepish grin, he opened the box. "I've kept it in the glove box since you gave it back." He plucked the engagement ring from the velvet confines. "Will you marry me?"

Tear blurred her view of the token. "Just try to stop me."

He smiled and slipped the ring onto her finger and drew her close, sealing the engagement with a heart-stopping kiss.

Relief flooded her. Peace. Contentment.

They sat on the swing, hand-in-hand, and watched the sky switch from blue to shades of pink and orange and finally gray. As she watched the sunset in all of its stages, Esther marveled at the perfection of God's timing.

She laid her head on Tom's shoulder and sighed when he kissed her head.

Her heart rested, knowing that her life was ordered along with nature. That God's love for her had planned her course and had given her the man of her dreams. The rest of her life would play out—in His time.

epilogue

"Breathe, Esther! One-two-three."

"I *am* breathing! Otherwise I'd be dead." There came a time in a woman's life—childbirth for instance—when she didn't need anyone telling her to breathe. If Tom didn't get out of her face in about two and a half seconds, she was going to send him from the room. His nervous energy was driving her nuts.

She cast a pleading glance at Ashley. The girl smiled. "Dad, Esther is only in early stages of labor. Natural breathing will get her through for now. Let's go get some coffee."

Coffee? That's all she needed—Tom strung out on a stimulant. She shook her head vigorously at the girl.

"Uh, on second thought, maybe caffeine isn't a good idea. We'll get you some milk or something."

"I can't leave my wife," he insisted. "What if she needs something?"

"I have the nurse's call button right here, sweetheart," Esther said quickly. "It might be a good idea for you to get some calories in you now. Later I'll need you by my side."

He bent and kissed her. "Are you sure?"

"Positive."

"I've been a pain, haven't I?" He sent her a sheepish grin.

She patted his cheek. "Only mildly. But I love you for it."

"All right. I'm going for awhile. Have me paged if you need me."

"I will. I promise."

Ashley sent her a wink and herded the prospective new

father from the room, leaving Esther to breathe on her own.

The phone rang next to the bed. Maneuvering her IV, she snatched up the receiver. "Hello?"

Minnie's voice groused over the line. "He wouldn't go to sleep without saying good night to you."

"Put him on."

"Mommy?"

Esther's heart soared at the sound of her four-year-old son's voice.

"Yes, baby. I'm so glad you called."

"Is Hannah here yet?"

"Not yet, but soon. Probably by the time you wake up tomorrow, you'll have a little sister. Won't that be fun?"

"Yes."

"Okay, I want you to go to bed now. I love you."

"I love you, too. Night."

Shortly after she and Tom married, Karen had called needing a foster home for the child. Afraid to risk her heart again, Esther's initial response was to decline. But after prayer, she and Tom both felt the Lord's leading to take Jason into their home. God worked out the circumstances and, within a year, plans were in progress to adopt the child of her heart.

She felt a tightening in her abdomen, accompanied by the telltale pain of labor—bearable, but stronger than before. Closing her eyes until the contraction ended, she concentrated on breathing. It wouldn't be long now before this child joined their family. A miracle. She and Tom had decided God's perfect plan was for them to adopt Jason and be content with raising one child together. But God had other ideas.

Before Jason's adoption was even final, she'd discovered she was pregnant.

The pregnancy went off without a hitch and now they were down to the final stage.

One thing she'd learned in the last two years was that her course truly wasn't hers to set—that God had a perfect plan, a purpose, and timing.

Eight hours later, as she lay nursing her beautiful baby daughter, she knew without a doubt that God's timing had produced a life for her that all her struggle and manipulation never could have.

She glanced to the vinyl chair next to the bed and smiled at Tom, whose chest rose and fell in light sleep. As if summoned by her perusal, he opened his eyes and gave her a lazy smile. "Are you okay?" he asked, his voice husky from sleep.

"Wonderful. Go back to sleep."

"Love you," he mumbled even as his eyelids drifted downward once again.

"Love you, too," she whispered.

She leaned back against her pillow and closed her eyes. Contentment eased through her exhaustion and she smiled. God had made all of her dreams a reality. In His time.

A Letter To Our Readers

Dear Reader:

In order that we might better contribute to your reading enjoyment, we would appreciate your taking a few minutes to respond to the following questions. We welcome your comments and read each form and letter we receive. When completed, please return to the following:

Fiction Editor
Heartsong Presents
PO Box 719
Uhrichsville, Ohio 44683

1. Did you enjoy reading *Timing Is Everything* by Tracey V. Bateman?
   ☐ Very much! I would like to see more books by this author!
   ☐ Moderately. I would have enjoyed it more if

   _____

   _____

   _____

2. Are you a member of **Heartsong Presents**? ☐ Yes ☐ No
   If no, where did you purchase this book? _____

   _____

3. How would you rate, on a scale from 1 (poor) to 5 (superior), the cover design? _____

4. On a scale from 1 (poor) to 10 (superior), please rate the following elements.

   ____ Heroine   ____ Plot
   ____ Hero   ____ Inspirational theme
   ____ Setting   ____ Secondary characters

5. These characters were special because?_____
_____
_____

6. How has this book inspired your life?_____
_____
_____

7. What settings would you like to see covered in future
Heartsong Presents books? _____
_____
_____

8. What are some inspirational themes you would like to see
treated in future books? _____
_____
_____

9. Would you be interested in reading other **Heartsong
Presents** titles? ❏ Yes ❏ No

10. Please check your age range:
   ❏ Under 18   ❏ 18-24
   ❏ 25-34   ❏ 35-45
   ❏ 46-55   ❏ Over 55

Name_____
Occupation _____
Address _____
City_____ State_____ Zip_____

MICHIGAN

4 stories in 1

Four couples come together in diverse Michigan locations, but they each have to answer the same question: Will they allow God to lead in thier love lives?

Author Gail Gaymer Martin shares her love of her home state and God in these four romances filled with faith, humor, adventure, and suspense.

Historical, paperback, 464 pages, 5 $\frac{3}{16}$"x 8"

Heartsong

Presents